CW00621502

Jasmine

by

Mirabelle Maslin

Augur Press

JASMINE
Copyright © Mirabelle Maslin 2015
The moral right of the author has been asserted

Author of: Beyond the Veil
Tracy
Carl and other writings
Fay
On a Dog Lead
Emily
The Fifth Key
The Candle Flame
The Supply Teacher's Surprise
Miranda
Lynne
Field Fare
Lentigo Maligna Melanoma
Infants and children: Emotional development

British Library Cataloguing in Publication Data.
A catalogue record for this book is available from
the British Library.

ISBN 978-0-9571380-9-4
First published 2015 by
Augur Press
Delf House
52 Penicuik Road
Roslin
Midlothian EH25 9LH
United Kingdom

Printed by Lightning Source

Jasmine

For Sue Lowman

Chapter One

To Jasmine, life felt full of promise. She had worked hard at school and had secured her longed-for place at university to do business studies. It had been great to be so near to uni. Fifteen minutes' quick walking, and she was there.

There had been no question of living away from home. Some of her friends went away to study. She didn't envy them. Not at all. Staying at home for those years meant that she could keep her living costs to a minimum, and in any case, leaving her family was unthinkable. She had always spent a lot of time with her younger brothers, Norrie and Blake. Norrie and Blake were twins, and to the untrained eye they appeared identical. Then there was her 'baby' sister, Poppy. She and Poppy had hardly anything in common, but Jasmine had always loved her and had always been deeply involved in her upbringing. Poppy had been about to start high school, and Jasmine could never imagine not being there to see what she made of it.

Jasmine had different colouring from her siblings. They were quite fair whereas she was dark – dark hair, dark eyes and dark skin. There had been some mention of a Peruvian ancestor on Mum's side of the family, but Jasmine had never really taken much notice of this, so hadn't absorbed the details. She was of average height, with broad shoulders and a sturdy body, whereas her siblings were slender. Norrie and Blake looked as if they might end up being quite tall. Jasmine often thought that if they filled out later on, they might turn out looking rather like Dad. Poppy had started life as a smallish baby, but had had spells of growing very fast, and at this stage it was difficult to guess what height she might reach as an adult. In general, she looked not unlike

Mum.

Everyone liked Jasmine. She had a cheerful personality, and would give a helping hand to anyone who needed it. She always had plenty of friends, and she liked going out with them, but most of all she loved being at home with her family. Mum and Dad were wonderful people, and home was full of fun and laughter.

One of Jasmine's main interests was troubleshooting computer problems. In fact, she was passionate about this. Friends and acquaintances were forever phoning to get her input on this or that glitch. Jasmine always answered these calls good-naturedly. No, it was far more than that. She had a special excitement and a gleam in her eyes whenever she was diagnosing the root of their problems. Norrie and Blake loved repairing computers, and although only fifteen, their skills were very advanced. Mum and Dad used to smile when they saw Norrie, Blake and Jasmine discussing plans for the next phase of their joint researches, and Dad spoke of how he imagined the advancement of burgeoning business ventures in the not-too-distant future.

The family had been completed by the addition of a small stray cat which had come into their lives on Poppy's fifth birthday. He had simply strolled in and made his home with them, as if it were where he should have been from the start. He had a habit of curling up wherever and whenever he fancied – whether it was on a bed, on someone's knee or in a box or basket. You only had to look at him and he would start to purr loudly, exposing his tummy to be stroked and tickled. He was black with a few small areas of white, one of which was at the end of his tail. It was because of this unusual feature that they called him Tippy.

If Jasmine were honest with herself, she had to admit that uni had turned out to be quite a struggle, and in the end she only just scraped through her degree exams. After this she knew that finding work might not be all that easy, and after some

2

thought and discussion she decided to spend a year at college doing a course in office management. She took to it like a duck to water, and gained very high marks in every module. This left her feeling happy, confident and fulfilled. Although the job market had shrunk considerably over the previous eighteen months, she believed that her range of skills meant that she would get some appropriate kind of work. A temporary post or something part-time would do for a start. She made contact with the three main recruitment agencies in town, and was soon preparing for their assessment interviews.

Despite the fact that she tested as being well above average, she was warned that local work might be hard to find. From then on, she put all her daytime energies into looking in the local Job Centre and scrutinising the relevant columns in the newspapers. In the evenings she worked as a relief waitress at a restaurant in the centre of town so that she could pay her share of the household expenses.

Several months passed. Then Jasmine saw an advertisement in the *Evening News*:

> *Person required for temporary post*
> *– full-time secretarial duties.*
> *Contact Mr Moran at Snaith and Drew, Solicitors.*

There was an address and a phone number. Although it was early evening, she rang the number straight away. A recorded message told her to leave contact details and an application form would be sent out. Aware that even this action could contribute to the firm's assessment of her, she spoke clearly and confidently, taking care to include her e-mail address. If they e-mailed the form to her the following morning, she could fill it in straight away. Their office was on the other side of town, but transport would not be a problem, as she knew that a good bus service passed only ten minutes' walk from where she lived.

To her great delight, she received an e-mail early the next day. A form was attached, and she soon completed it. She wanted to send it off immediately, but common sense prevailed. She decided that she would go out for a stroll to mull things over. She wished that she could ask Dad to look through it with her, but he wasn't going to be home until late that night, and she was determined to send it to Snaith and Drew by the end of the working day at the very latest. As she walked, thoughts about more information to put on the form came into her mind, and she rushed back to the house to include it. After that, she corrected a few minor errors, took a very deep breath and sent the form off.

Exactly one week later, Jasmine received an e-mail from Snaith and Drew. Her hand trembling, she opened it.

'I've got an interview!' she shouted to the empty house. She grabbed her mobile and quickly wrote a text to send to both Dad and Mum. After that she put her mind to the practicalities. 'Thursday today. Interview on Monday morning. Not long to wait,' she murmured. 'Maybe I could buy something new to wear?' That seemed a very good idea, and she spent much of the afternoon searching the shops for something smart but inexpensive.

By luck, she found an end-of-line suit that was exactly her size and was a shade of brown that was perfect for her. She came across some nice dark nut-brown shoes that had been reduced in price because of a minor blemish. Finding that they looked good on her and were very comfortable, she snapped them up. Then she realised that she could complete the outfit with the cream-coloured blouse she had found in last year's sales. Content, she returned home with her purchases.

The weekend brought with it an opportunity to show her interview attire off to the whole family. Mum and Dad were very supportive, assuring her that she had made good choices. Poppy said the suit didn't look right, but then she admitted that she was jealous because Jasmine looked so smart and was soon having a job interview. After that she changed her view of the suit and said it looked brilliant. However, Norrie and Blake reacted in a way that to Jasmine was entirely inexplicable. They sat and talked to each other and ignored her completely. It was as if she didn't exist. She hadn't particularly expected them to be interested in her clothes, but their apparent lack of interest in what she was preparing for was quite unexpected, and hurtful.

Then Dad noticed that although Jasmine was doing her best to hide it, she was looking a bit upset, and he guessed why.

He addressed Norrie and Blake. 'Come on, you two. You'll have to accept that your big sister has to push out into the big wide world. Give her a bit of support. It'll be you next, and you'll expect her to say the right things to you then.'

'That's just it,' Blake grumbled. 'I like it here with the three of us and our projects, but the writing's on the wall, and our days together are numbered,' he added dramatically.

'Exactly my sentiments,' said Norrie mournfully.

'Oh no!' Poppy complained. 'I don't want to think about *all* of you going away. I'll be left on my own, with only Tippy for company.' She pulled the sides of her mouth down as far as she could.

'All I'm doing is trying to get a job. I'm not moving to the other side of the world,' Jasmine said crossly.

'Come on now, boys.' Dad spoke with mock sternness. 'Put some effort into saying something useful.'

Norrie and Blake glared at him. 'We were!' they said together.

Jasmine rushed to defend them. 'Dad, it's just their way of saying they'll miss me when I'm out of the house more.'

'That's right,' Norrie agreed.

5

'Yeah,' added Blake.

Norrie went on. 'And anyway, she knows she looks great in that gear.'

Blake nodded. 'She doesn't need us to tell her.'

Jasmine smiled. 'Thanks for the compliments. I'll go and get changed, and then we can get on with the backlog of computer questions that have been flooding in recently.'

Chapter Two

Jasmine set off early on Monday morning. It was a breezy October day, although it was quite mild, and there was no sign of rain. The interview was to be at 10 o'clock, and she wanted to arrive in plenty of time. She was keen to have a look round the neighbouring streets and familiarise herself with the outside of the office before going in.

It was nine thirty when she stepped off the bus at the end of the road. She felt a stirring of excitement as she identified the address, and then walked on. It looked as if the offices of Snaith and Drew were on the ground floor of what had once been a substantial family dwelling. As she walked she saw that she was passing similarly large stone-built detached properties, many of which appeared to have been converted into flats or offices. Each building had enough ground at the front for car parking and a few ornamental shrubs.

When she came to a crossroads she turned left and found herself in a street where there were neat red-brick terraced houses on one side, and on the other was a row of tiny bungalows. The bungalows puzzled her until she realised that they must have been purpose-built for older people. A further left turn meant that she was in a road that was parallel to her destination, and one more left turn brought her to where she had left the bus. It was now ten to ten. Jasmine decided that it was time to go to the office and introduce herself.

A large brass plate on the stone frontage of the building reassured her that she had indeed reached the offices of Snaith and Drew. A sign beside the heavy glass door instructed her to press the buzzer, which she did without hesitation. A man's voice spoke to her through the intercom, and she told him that she was Jasmine Simmons and that she had an appointment to see Mr Moran at ten o'clock. There was a click as the door catch released, and she went in.

A man appeared in the entrance hall and introduced himself as Mr Moran. He was formally dressed in a black suit with a dark tie and black shoes. Jasmine guessed that he must be about the same age as her dad – around fifty – about the same height, but thinner.

'You're a little early, Ms Simmons,' he remarked, 'but as you're the first on the list, we can make a start immediately. Please come this way.' He opened a door at the side of the hall. Then he led Jasmine into a small room that had only a desk and some chairs in it.

Jasmine smiled. She felt comfortable with this person. His manner was precise and straightforward.

'Please take a seat,' he invited. 'I'll be back in a few minutes.'

He disappeared out of the door, leaving Jasmine to contemplate what lay ahead of her. She thought about everything that she remembered putting in her application. She had no idea how many other people were to be interviewed. She knew that she must not ask, although she dearly wanted to know.

When Mr Moran returned, he had a woman with him, who to Jasmine seemed to be of a similar age.

'Sorry to keep you waiting,' he said politely. 'This is Mrs Reid. She'll be sitting in with us.'

Jasmine stood up and shook hands with the woman, who was carrying two folders, one of which she then placed on the desk. Mr Moran sat behind the desk, with Mrs Reid to his left. They opened the folders, and he began.

'Ms Simmons, I should first explain that there has been a change.'

Jasmine immediately began to feel anxious. She said nothing, and waited.

Mr Moran continued. 'We had intended to conduct

formal interviews today, but because of unforeseen circumstances we have made the decision to meet applicants in a less formal way. As you will know from the documentation we provided with the application form, our intention was to recruit someone to cover for nine months.'

Jasmine nodded. Her heart was beating quickly. She wished that he would get to the point.

'We have had to reduce that period to four months, and before we go any further, we have to ask if you're still interested in the post.'

'Yes, of course I am,' Jasmine assured him eagerly. Four months of experience in a place like this would be a good start. 'Yes,' she repeated, 'definitely.'

'We won't need to keep you for long today,' he told her. 'Having considered your application, there are only a few points I want to raise.'

Mentally, Jasmine crossed her fingers, but her hands lay motionless on her lap.

'We need someone who can work overtime at fairly short notice. Will that be a problem for you?'

'Not at all,' Jasmine told him confidently. She knew that she would be happy to work long hours if necessary. 'I'd be able to start early or finish late on most days. I don't live too far away and the bus service is very good,' she explained.

'You have a useful combination of qualifications,' mused Mr Moran. 'And I see that you have a particular interest in computer troubleshooting.'

'That's correct,' Jasmine replied. In her eagerness and enthusiasm she rushed on to say, 'I just love it, and I'm pretty good at it as well.' Too late she realised her mistake and she felt her cheeks redden. 'I mean...' Here she almost stuttered. 'I... I've built up some informal experience.' She could no longer look at him, and instead looked past him at the wall behind his seat.

Mr Moran appeared as if he had not noticed her state of

confusion, and commented, as if to himself, 'That could come in handy.' He paused before continuing. 'We are a very busy practice. There are three partners – myself, Mrs Reid, and one other. In addition we have a legal assistant and a trainee. We have one full-time secretary, Mrs Cowan, who has been with us for many years. If your application is successful, you will be working directly under her.' He turned to Mrs Reid. 'Is there anything you want to ask?'

'We need to know how soon you would be able to start.'

'Thank you,' said Mr Moran. He turned to Jasmine and waited.

Jasmine thought quickly. She didn't want to leave the restaurant in the lurch, but she wanted these people to think that she could be available as soon as they needed. She was desperate to get this job. The whole feel of the place was good, and the experience of working here would be invaluable. Then the perfect answer came to her.

'I have evening responsibilities for the next two weeks, but apart from that I'm free to start as soon as you want.' In any case, she thought, she could still do weekend cover for the waitressing beyond that if the restaurant needed her. Friday and Saturday nights were nearly always the busiest.

Mr Moran smiled at her. 'Thank you for stating that so clearly, and thank you for your time.' He stood up, came round the front of the desk, and shook her hand warmly. Then he showed her out saying, 'We'll be in touch with you within seven working days.'

As she walked back along the road to the bus stop, Jasmine was filled with a curious mixture of calm and agitation. Before this day, she could not have imagined having this combination of feelings, but now it consumed her. Before, she could have seen no logic in that mix, yet now it seemed entirely to be expected. The calm came from experiencing the good atmosphere in that place, and the agitation was from her desperation to work there but having to wait to find out. Fleetingly she felt driven to rush back and hammer on the door, begging them to give her the day and time when she would know. However, being crystal clear that such behaviour would wreck any chance of being employed there, she took the next bus home.

That evening, Norrie and Blake tried their best to dig information out of Jasmine, but she wouldn't be drawn. Poppy was more careful in her approach, but she, too, failed to divine anything. Later, Jasmine managed to get a private chat in the kitchen with her parents while the others were fighting about who was going in the shower first.

Her dad gave her a hug and was reassuring. 'From what you've told us you did very well. It was good you let them see how keen you are on computers.'

'Maybe,' replied Jasmine, 'but I wish I hadn't done it quite like that. I must have sounded like a schoolgirl.'

'Try not to worry,' her mother soothed. 'You never know. That kind of fresh enthusiasm might have counted in your favour.'

Jasmine considered this for a moment. 'I never thought of it that way,' she conceded.

Her mother went on. 'Now don't you lose any sleep over it. And remember, they're fools if they decide not to give you the job.'

Jasmine smiled. 'Thanks for that vote of confidence, Mum.'

Chapter Three

The following days were difficult. Jasmine cleaned the house from top to bottom in an attempt to numb the endless circling question in her head about whether or not she was going to be offered the job. She couldn't face going to check what was available at the Job Centre. The only job she wanted was the one with Snaith and Drew. The evenings were easier because she was concentrating hard on customers' orders at the restaurant, and on holding conversations that would enhance their enjoyment of the food. At night she would collapse into bed and fall asleep quite quickly, only to dream of the office, and of herself gazing longingly through the heavy glass door.

Thursday afternoon came, and having exhausted all the housework possibilities, Jasmine decided to take herself for a walk in the park. It was while she was crumbling a biscuit on to the ground for a grey squirrel that her mobile phone rang.

'Hang on a minute, squirrel,' she said, 'I'd better see who this is.' She pulled her phone out of her pocket and replied. 'Hi, this is Jasmine.'

She heard a formal voice say 'Hello Ms Simmons. This is Mrs Reid from Snaith and Drew. We met on Monday.'

Oh no, thought Jasmine. I never imagined they might ring me. I thought it would be an e-mail or a letter. 'Er... Hello, Mrs Reid,' she said uncertainly.

'I'm contacting you to let you know that we've sent you a formal offer of the temporary post of secretarial support. There's a letter in the post, but we've also sent an e-mail. Will you be able to let us know by Monday?'

'I can let you know now!' exclaimed Jasmine happily. 'The answer's yes, and I'll start as soon as you want.' Oh no! she thought. What have I done? You're not supposed to talk like this under such circumstances. She broke into a sweat. The squirrel was nibbling at a crumb on her shoe, but she didn't notice. All she was aware of was the feeling that her whole future was hanging in the balance. Then she heard Mrs Reid's voice again.

'You'll see on the job offer that we've asked if you can start a week on Monday. However, if you can begin sooner than that, please let us know.'

Jasmine wanted to shout that she would start the very next day, but she managed to contain herself and instead said, 'I'm sure I'll be able to arrange that. I'll give an exact date in my e-mail reply.' That sounded better... much better.

'On behalf of Snaith and Drew, I can say that we will look forward to you joining us,' Mrs Reid finished.

Jasmine was euphoric. To the surprise of the squirrel, she jumped high into the air. 'I've got it!' she shouted to no one. Although the squirrel had retreated several feet it had not run away. 'Squirrel, we've got to celebrate,' Jasmine told it breathlessly. 'I'll go and get something nice to share. You wait here, and I'll be back soon.'

It was only four o'clock and none of her family would be at home yet. She longed to tell her parents, but she would have to wait. Sending texts didn't feel right. She wanted to tell them in person.

She jogged to a local shop, bought a packet of mixed nuts, and hurried back to the spot where she had left her animal friend, but it was nowhere to be seen. Feeling disappointed, she sat on a nearby bench and opened the bag. Examining the contents she found walnuts, hazelnuts, brazils, pecans, cashews and some peanuts. 'Excellent variety,' she murmured.

It was then that she became aware of movement at the

other end of the bench, and there was a squirrel, watching her closely. She had no idea whether or not this was the same one, but it hardly mattered. Carefully she laid out a row of the nuts half way along the bench. Quickly the squirrel jumped forward, grabbed one and retreated to the far end, where it sat, holding the nut between its paws and gnawing at it. Jasmine was content, and she relaxed for a while in the companionship of her small friend before walking back home briskly to look for the expected e-mail.

When she arrived, she found Poppy sitting in the kitchen with a bowl of muesli in front of her. 'I'm hungry,' she stated.

'And I've got the job!' Jasmine told her excitedly.

Poppy dropped her spoon into the bowl. 'Really? Really, really?'

'Yes, really. Mrs Reid, she's one of the partners, phoned me on my mobile and said I would get an e-mail and a letter.'

'Wow! I've got a sister with a proper job.' Poppy jumped to her feet and gave Jasmine a big hug. 'I'm sorry I haven't been nice to you about your job hunting.'

'It's okay. Is Mum back yet?'

'Yes, but she went out again. I can't remember where she was going, but she's not far away.'

'I'll go and check my e-mails.'

'I'm coming, too,' said Poppy. 'I want to see.'

Minutes later they were viewing the message from Snaith and Drew.

'It's really grown up,' Poppy remarked.

Jasmine chuckled. 'There would be something very wrong if it weren't. Now, I'm going to draft a reply, but I won't send it off straight away.'

Poppy was puzzled. 'Why not?'

'The office will be closed now. I'll send it off later this evening, after I've spoken to Mum and Dad. It's good to talk this kind of thing over with someone who's done it all before.'

Poppy took this in. 'Oh, I see... Oof, there's a lot to grasp about this whole business.'

Jasmine found herself hovering by the front door, waiting for her mother to return. She felt like a small child who was bursting with her news.

At last she heard a key in the lock. She flung the door open only to find that it was Norrie and Blake.

'Oh!' she exclaimed.

'Don't sound so excited to see us,' said Norrie with a grin.

'I thought it was Mum.'

'Perhaps I should return with a different hairstyle?' Blake suggested.

Jasmine shoved him affectionately as he went past her. 'By the way, I've got the job,' she added matter-of-factly.

'You haven't!' said Norrie, his eyes open wide.

'Oh yes, I have.' She turned to close the door, saw her mother coming through the gate, and ran down the path to meet her. 'I've got it! I've got the job!'

Her mother was delighted. 'Well done! Have you told your dad yet? He'll be so excited.'

'He's not back.'

'I know, but you could give him a ring.'

'Maybe I'll send him a text soon.'

'We must have a celebration,' her mother announced. 'What shall we have for tea?'

'I shared a packet of nuts with a squirrel in the park,' Jasmine told her, 'but I'd love a mountain of your curry and rice this evening. Everyone likes it. I'll give you a hand to make it.'

They were busy in the kitchen when Dad came home.

'Guess what?' she told him as he came in to see them.

'What?' he replied, feigning ignorance.

'I got the job.'

His face broke into a broad smile. 'That's excellent!

Jasmine, I'm so proud of you.' He came across and gave her a hug.

'Watch out!' she warned. 'You'll get covered in curry sauce.'

'That won't deter me,' he said. 'This is a very important occasion.'

Later that evening, Jasmine sat with her mum and dad, and read out the e-mail from Snaith and Drew, together with her planned reply.

'Perfect! Send it off straight away,' her dad told her.

Jasmine hesitated.

'Your dad's right,' her mum said. 'Go on!'

Needing no further encouragement, Jasmine sent off her message. Then she was filled with a wonderful warm feeling, and she relaxed.

Chapter Four

Jasmine soon found that working at Snaith and Drew was a real joy. It did not take her long to get to know the people and to understand the office systems. Her IT skills were put to very good use, and she learned that in addition to her other qualifications, her special interest in IT was what had made her stand out as the preferred candidate. Four months of this kind of experience would surely lead to a good reference that she could use for other job applications.

Life felt very good.

It was just after the first three weeks of Jasmine's new life that the blow fell. Her dad was made redundant. Normally cheerful and energetic, he became quiet and often looked worried. He spent long hours searching for potential work and filling in application forms. Jasmine did everything she could think of to help, but although he was appreciative, nothing helped his mood.

Jasmine continued to flourish at work, and apart from her own good feelings about this, she could see that her dad was pleased she was making a lot of progress in a relatively short time. He was clearly proud of her.

Then came the day when things changed. Jasmine arrived home one day to discover that her dad was almost back to his old self.

'It looks as if I've got something,' he told her.

'That's great, Dad!' she replied, but she was surprised to see that Mum looked quite subdued. 'What is it, Mum?' she asked.

'In these difficult times, this news is wonderful, but

there is a downside.' She looked across at her husband. 'Shall I tell her, or do you want to?'

'I'd better be the one,' he replied. 'After all, it's because of me that it's happening.'

Jasmine was puzzled. What were they talking about? Dad had a job again. What was the problem?

'We'll have to move,' he informed her bluntly.

'Move?' Jasmine echoed. Surely that couldn't be true. She had lived in this house ever since she was born. Nothing had changed except that along the way she had gained two brothers and a sister.

Her dad went on. 'The job's at least a good four hours' drive from here – that's when the roads are clear – and I'll need to be around outside working hours.' He paused before adding, 'It's an opportunity that in the current economic climate I can't give up. It's a full-time permanent post, and if I really go at it, there might even be promotion.'

Here her mother continued the story. 'We've talked about getting somewhere for your dad to live during the working week, coming home at weekends. But it's just not going to suit because to make the best of this chance, he must be nearby more or less all the time.'

'Have you told the others yet?' asked Jasmine quickly.

'We thought we'd tell you first,' her mother explained. 'We'll tell the others after tea.'

Jasmine looked at her watch. 'Shall we make a start on the meal?' she asked, longing for something practical to get on with while she tried to absorb the news.

She and her mother worked side by side while Dad continued with the property search that he had already begun on the internet.

Peeling carrots studiedly, Jasmine said quietly, 'I'll look for a place in a shared flat.'

'You probably won't need to,' her mother replied. 'It'll take us a while to sell this and find somewhere else, and you'll have finished your job before we move.'

'But all my friends are here,' Jasmine murmured, almost to herself. She turned to her mother and added, 'I could come and see you at weekends.'

'It's a long journey,' her mother reminded her.

Jasmine fell silent. She could hardly even begin to imagine what the change would be like. As she and her mother worked together to prepare the meal, they spoke only about the recipe that they were following.

It was not long before there was a crash at the front door, followed by the sound of it being slammed shut, and then Blake and Norrie appeared in the kitchen.

'We're hungry,' they announced together.

Jasmine winked at her mother. 'So are we,' she informed them.

'You could lay the table,' Mum suggested.

To Jasmine's surprise, her brothers did not complain. Instead, they grabbed cutlery and mats and arranged them on the table in the dining area, where they sat having a heated argument about who was going to get the water jug and glasses.

When the food was nearly ready, Jasmine called up the stairs to Poppy, who was doing her homework in her room.

It was while they were seated round the table that Dad told the others that he had some news.

'Gr…ea…t!' said Blake, his mouth full of potato.

'What is it?' asked Norrie. He was in the process of getting up from his chair, and he wasn't sure whether he needed to sit down again.

Poppy was concentrating on trying to conceal the fact that she was slipping fragments of chicken to Tippy, who was hiding on her knee.

Jasmine poked her leg. 'You'd better listen,' she told her, 'it's important.'

'I've got a new job,' Dad told them.

'That was quick,' Norrie commented. 'The dad of one of my mates was out of work for more than a year.'

'Yes, it's a lot sooner than I imagined.'

Norrie stood up fully and started to leave.

'You'll need to stay for a bit,' Dad said. 'There's more you need to know.'

Norrie sat down again. 'You'll have to make it quick,' he mumbled, 'I've a lot to see to.'

'We'll have to move house,' said Dad bluntly.

Blake swallowed loudly and sat bolt upright. 'Why?' he demanded.

'The new job's far too far away for me to commute, and in any case I'll need to work a lot of extra hours, so I'll have to be close by.'

Blake and Norrie gaped at each other in dismay and moaned loudly. 'That means we'll have to move school.'

By this time, Poppy's attention was fully on the subject under discussion. For now, Tippy had been forgotten. 'I've only just started mine,' she protested.

'It's going to be quite an upheaval for all of us,' said Mum, 'but Dad and I are certain we're doing the right thing.'

'I think I'll have to stay here,' said Jasmine quietly.

The twins swivelled their heads round and gaped at her. 'But you can't!'

She continued. 'I don't mean here, in this house. I'll look for a room in a shared flat.' Then she saw panic in Poppy's eyes, and added hastily, 'I'll come and visit you all.'

There was complete silence for at least a minute.

'Look, you three,' said Jasmine firmly. 'A change of school won't be the end of the world. In fact, it might bring more opportunities for you all.'

Jasmine's heart was aching. She couldn't imagine life without seeing her family nearly every day. She told herself that she was just going to have to discover what that life was *and* make the best of it. Secretly, she hoped that there would be more work for her at Snaith and Drew after the four months there. She hadn't said this to anyone yet, not even Mum.

20

For the rest of the evening, the house was strangely quiet. Norrie and Blake went off to their room, and Poppy sat on a chair by the gas fire in the sitting room with Tippy on her knee, stroking him studiedly. Jasmine busied herself doing the washing up and tidying the kitchen, while Mum and Dad looked at houses together on the internet.

Chapter Five

Jasmine began her research about accommodation straight away. At the moment she had no idea of the cost of a room in a flat, or quite where she wanted to aim for, but it seemed obvious that the more she found out now, the better.

She contacted two of her friends who lived in rented rooms, and fixed a meeting with each of them. She had known Freya since they were at primary school together, and Maider had come into her life during her university days.

Freya's father was in the army, and so her parents had moved around a lot, but Freya had lived with her granny during term time, so that she didn't keep having to move to different schools. Maider's parents were Spanish, and her colouring was darker than Jasmine's. Jasmine had met Maider's parents once and had liked them instantly, but very sadly indeed, they had died in a terrible car accident when she and Maider were in their second year at uni.

Freya was by now a qualified nurse, and she lived in a modest flat in the centre of town, which she shared with two other people. Jasmine had been there many times, and liked the flat. Freya had been there for several years, but the other occupants never stayed for long, as they were either on short-term work contracts or were overseas students studying on short courses. Although the flat itself was pleasant, Jasmine didn't like the location, as it was very near to a busy pub. This didn't seem to bother Freya, so Jasmine never remarked on it. She had no idea how much Freya paid to live there, as there had never before been any reason to discuss costs.

When Freya learned of Jasmine's situation, she immediately suggested that they spend an evening together at the flat to talk things through, so Monday evening saw Jasmine climbing the flight of stairs to the first floor of the block. Almost as soon as she knocked on the door of the flat, Freya opened it.

'Hi!' she greeted Jasmine with a broad smile. 'It's great to see you. Come on in.'

Jasmine stepped into the small hallway, saying, 'It's good of you to meet up so soon.'

'I've been missing you,' Freya told her, 'and so I grabbed at the opportunity to see you. By the way, this week's ideal for our chat about flats because I'm alone at the moment. The other rooms are between tenants, so for the first time I can show you round the whole place. The next occupants are due to arrive on Saturday.' She shuddered dramatically. 'I hope they don't gnaw at the ends of chicken legs like the others did.'

Jasmine pulled a funny face, and then sniffed the air. 'I can smell something interesting wafting from the kitchen.'

'Certainly not chicken legs, but I've put something together that I hope you'll find tempting.' Freya glanced at her watch. 'Should be ready in about forty-five minutes. Tell you what, I'll show you the other bedrooms, and then we'll sit down and make a start on your list of questions.'

Jasmine found that these rooms were similar in size to the one that Freya used. The only difference was that one of them had a sink in a corner near the window.

They sat down in the comfortable living area that adjoined the kitchen.

'Fire away, then,' Freya told her friend.

'Do you mind telling me how much you have to pay for living here?'

'Not at all. It's fifty pounds a week plus my share of the gas and electricity bills. The landline has been disconnected because in the last few years no one has ever wanted to use it. Like me, everyone uses a mobile all the time.'

Jasmine took a small notebook and a pen out of her bag

and started jotting notes.

'Do you know how old this building is?' she asked. 'I guess it's relatively modern.'

'You're right. I think it was built in the late '60s. Why do you ask?'

'The ceilings are quite low.'

'In the winter that can be an advantage because the rooms need less heat to be warm enough.'

Jasmine nodded. She felt a bit embarrassed because she had never considered that sort of thing before. She paid her parents fifty pounds a week, and that covered everything, including food.

'Who owns the flat?' she asked.

'I'm not sure. The let is administered through an agent in town, and I think the owners live abroad. In any case, I deal entirely with the agent. I've been here for nearly five years, and I've never had any difficulty. All the appliances are checked regularly by qualified tradespeople. If any problem crops up, all I have to do is ring the agent or pop into the office, and whatever it is gets fixed promptly. For example, drips started coming in through my window when it was raining heavily, and someone fixed it the next day.'

'Freya, it's really useful to know all this,' said Jasmine gratefully. 'I'm learning a lot already about the sort of things to look out for and the kind of questions to ask.' She made a few more notes.

'What's next?' asked Freya.

'Why have you stayed in this flat for years, while everyone else comes and goes? Surely that must be a bit disturbing. You've hardly got time to get to know people before they're off again.'

'Well, that's an interesting subject. Do you want the short answer or the longer one?'

Jasmine smiled. 'Both, of course.'

'The short answer is that it's handy for the Infirmary. There are nurses' quarters in a block in the grounds, but I

24

didn't fancy being on-site all the time, and there's almost no difference in costs.'

Freya's answer seemed complete, and Jasmine felt puzzled that her friend had a longer explanation, which would now follow. She waited.

Freya continued. 'I've been thinking myself about why I keep on living here, and recently I realised two things. One is that my room is quite similar to my bedroom at Gran's house, and the other is that her house was near a pub.'

'Goodness!' exclaimed Jasmine. 'How interesting! What a coincidence.'

'Well, said Freya, 'I don't know about it being a coincidence. When I look back to my flat-hunting, I remember falling in love with this room straight away. It just seemed like home to me.'

'Mm...' mused Jasmine. She certainly remembered how upset Freya had been when her gran died, quite suddenly, soon after she had left secondary school. She hadn't wanted to go back to live with her family, and instead she had lived with friends while she decided what she was going to do. Her father had supplemented her meagre income until she was earning enough to manage. 'Freya, I wish I'd been more of a friend to you after your gran died, but I was all tied up with uni, and to be honest, I was floundering.'

'Don't beat yourself up about it,' Freya replied. 'I never thought that you weren't there for me. At that stage most of us were struggling along as best we could.' She glanced at her watch, and leapt to her feet. 'The food!' she exclaimed. 'I thought I detected a hint of a singeing smell in the air. We'd better serve it up, and resume our chatting later. I hope you like my concoction.'

Ten minutes later they were seated opposite each other at the kitchen table, each with a steaming plateful of what Freya referred to as 'slow risotto plus plus'.

'I've never heard of a dish by that name,' Jasmine

commented as she prepared to start eating.

Freya chuckled. 'I'm not surprised. It's my own invention.'

'The name or the recipe?'

'Both.'

Jasmine sampled a large forkful. 'Oh wow! It's wonderful! You *must* write out the recipe for me, and I'll make some at home for the others.'

'I don't exactly *have* a recipe,' Freya confessed. 'Each time is different.'

'But there must be some basic steps,' Jasmine stated.

'Oh yes, and I can easily write those down for you.'

Satisfied with this, Jasmine continued to work her way through Freya's delicious creation, while reminiscing about their days together at primary school.

'You came when we were both nearly eight, and I invited you to my birthday party.'

'That's right. I don't know how on earth your mum managed it all, because your brothers were only a few months old.'

Jasmine laughed. 'I remember her telling me that I could only have a birthday party that year if Dad would look after them, and I went on at him about it until in the end he promised. When I look back, Mum and Dad were brilliant. They probably were getting almost no sleep at the time, but they made sure I got my party.'

'And it was a good one, too,' said Freya. 'There were lots of really interesting games, and the food was amazing.'

'One of Mum's friends was a caterer. She came round early in the morning to help make the food, and her son, who seemed really grown up at fourteen, came later to help with the games.'

'And he did some really good conjuring tricks,' Freya added.

'Well remembered!' replied Jasmine.

They fell silent for a while, their minds drifting through

their memories of happy times together.

Then Jasmine continued. 'I remember how I thought it was so special that you went far away in the holidays. Everyone else in the class lived quite close by with their families, and you were the only one whose Mum and Dad were a long way away. I always missed you. The school holidays were okay, but going back to school meant that we could see each other again.'

'I always looked forward to seeing Mum and Dad again, but it meant being away from all my friends. It wasn't easy, and of course I didn't have any siblings.'

'Why didn't your parents come to stay with you at your gran's house in the holidays?' asked Jasmine suddenly.

'Dad had quite a responsible post. It was difficult for him to get away, and Mum didn't want to leave him on his own. The best thing was for me to go back to them.'

'I see,' Jasmine reflected, 'but it wasn't ideal for you.'

Freya looked straight at her friend. 'I think there isn't much in life that is ideal, and it's best to learn to be realistic about that as soon as possible.'

'You're right, of course,' Jasmine agreed. 'I think I was speaking from the primary school child part of me. Everyone was doing their best with a complicated situation. I was lucky that your parents decided to send you to your gran's to go to school, or I would never have met you.'

'Yes. Under the circumstances it was a very good choice. I don't know if I ever told you before, but from being age five to age eight I ended up going to four different primary schools.'

'Wow! No, you never told me that before.'

Freya stared at her. 'I've just realised something.'

'What's that?'

'You were asking me earlier how I felt about people never staying all that long in this flat.'

'Yes. If it were me, I'd definitely find it quite disturbing.'

'Well, I think I do, but because I've had a room that's so like the one I had at Gran's, I thought I was feeling okay. And of course, in a way, I am, but I can see now that that's not the whole story.'

Jasmine stared back at her friend. There was something she wanted to say, but she couldn't yet put words round it. 'Give me a minute to think,' she said.

But Freya continued, albeit speaking almost to herself. 'When I started school I had Mum, and Dad was coming and going. When we moved, I still had Mum, and Dad was still coming and going. *But the school and school friends kept changing.* When I was eight, I lived with Gran so my school didn't keep changing. Now I'm living here in a room like the one I had at Gran's *and my flatmates keep changing.*' She paused, and then stated, 'I don't remember anything much before I started primary school. When I next speak to Mum on the phone, I'm going to ask her how many times we moved before I was five.'

Jasmine had been struggling to follow everything that Freya was saying, but it certainly sounded logical. 'I agree that you should ask your mum about that,' she said emphatically. Then she added, 'I'm really impressed by your line of thought.'

'Well, I'm sure I wouldn't be having it if you hadn't been asking me questions about my life here,' Freya replied bluntly. She breathed out slowly, and then asked, 'Do you want some more to eat?'

'Delicious though it was, I haven't room for any more, thanks,' Jasmine replied. 'Why don't we tidy up the kitchen and then we can relax for the rest of the evening?'

'Good idea,' agreed Freya.

It was not long before they returned to the comfortable chairs in the living area to sip from mugs of hot green tea.

'Let me answer more of your questions about life in a rented flat,' Freya invited. 'Or maybe you'd like to say more about what's leading you towards branching out. You said on the phone that your family will soon move away, but you haven't yet explained why, and why you want to stay on here.'

Jasmine explained what she knew so far, and ended by saying that although the actual start date for Dad's new job was months away, it was important that he spent time there earlier than that, and that he and Mum were already looking at property on the internet.

'How far away are they moving?'

'It's around 200 miles from here.'

'Mm... so day-trip visits aren't going to be easy,' Freya mused.

'Absolutely not,' Jasmine agreed. 'Even if I could drive and had a car, it just wouldn't be feasible. On the front of staying here, I've worked out that I've got to branch out and make an independent life.' She paused for a moment and then added, 'If I go with them, Norrie and Blake might end up leaving home before I do!'

'I can see where you're coming from. What else is in your mind about it all?'

'Okay, now I'm going to tell you what's in my heart of hearts,' Jasmine confided. 'I'm hoping and hoping that I can get a full time permanent job at Snaith and Drew. I just *love* it there.'

Freya opened her mouth to say something, but Jasmine put up a hand to deter her.

'Oh, I know that it isn't very likely, and that's why I'm not saying anything to anyone else. The temporary post I have is only for four months.'

'I wasn't going to say that,' Freya objected. 'I was going to say that I sincerely hope your wish is fulfilled.'

Jasmine jumped up out of her seat and leaned over to hug her friend. 'Thank you so much!' she exclaimed. 'And that's enough about me for now. Tell me what your longer-term plans are. Is the Infirmary still where you want to be?'

'I didn't think we'd get a chance to talk about that this

29

evening, but now you mention it, there's quite a bit I'd like to mull over with you.'

'Well, go ahead. I'm all ears,' Jasmine encouraged.

'If there's more about flat hunting, we can cover it later,' said Freya.

'I can give you a ring some other time,' Jasmine replied cheerfully. 'We've made a good start, and now I want to hear more about *you*.'

Freya took a deep breath. 'So far, I've been sticking to general nursing. I've always liked the variety. I like the people I meet – staff and patients – and I've made lots of friends amongst staff I work with and from other parts of the hospital. It's all so very interesting. I'm always busy, and I like that. In fact, we're usually run off our feet! But...' Here Freya hesitated.

'But what?'

'In the last year I've found that nursing older people is what I find most satisfying.'

Jasmine was about to ask something else, but she could see that her friend was about to say more, so she waited.

'They are so interesting to talk to. Although everything is usually very busy, we can always have some chat while I'm doing whatever I have to do. I find their memories, and their views, attitudes and ideas fascinating. Of course, sometimes they are feeling low or grumpy, but when we start chatting, all that fades away, for then at least. And I can't wait to get back to continue with a line of thought or a memory.'

To Jasmine, Freya seemed to have entered a different kind of world. Her friend was still addressing her thoughts to her, but she was also being enriched by her experience as she recounted it.

'You sound really passionate about it,' Jasmine observed.

Freya considered this. 'I'm not sure about the passion,' she reflected. 'It's more a natural way of life. I'm sorry that these people are unwell and have to be in hospital, but I'm so lucky that they are, because it means that I can meet them all.'

Jasmine could tell that her friend was inspired by her experience, and she felt very happy for her. 'Are you going to move more into that kind of work?' she asked.

'I don't know,' Freya replied. 'I'm torn between staying in general nursing, where at the moment about twenty per cent of my work is with older people, or applying for a job in a specialist unit for care of the elderly, or perhaps working in a private care home.'

'I imagine you'll have to consider this very carefully,' said Jasmine. 'Working within a general hospital might have advantages you're not aware of.'

Freya was surprised. 'What do you mean?'

'Er... I don't know exactly. I'll have to think... It just came into my head, so I said it.' Jasmine sounded a little defensive.

Freya giggled. 'I'm not putting thumbscrews on you to deliver an explanation. I wanted to hear more because it's something I hadn't thought about. I've become so focused on whether to make a move and where that might take me that maybe I hadn't thought enough about what I'd be leaving behind. Jasmine, you are so wise.'

'I'm not sure about the "wise" bit. It can be easy to be like that about someone else's life, while completely missing significant things in my own,' Jasmine observed wryly.

'It looks as if we're both going to have to think carefully,' Freya commented.

'Yes, and the main thing for me is whether or not I'm going to let my family leave me behind here.'

'I don't see it quite like that,' Freya remarked. 'You were telling me that if you don't branch out now, you might end up being left behind at your parents' new home once your brothers and sister have gone. And anyway, you're giving off plenty of signs of someone who wants to branch out. Who knows, even if your family had been able to stay where they are, in a year's time, or less, you might have been looking for a room in a flat.'

When Jasmine considered this she knew that her friend was right.

'How about another drink?' Freya asked. 'I'm going to have one.'

Jasmine looked at her watch. 'Goodness!' she exclaimed. 'It's later than I thought. I'd better go. We both need our beauty sleep.'

'Why not have one more good look around the flat first?' Freya suggested. 'It's a golden opportunity while there's no one else here.'

Jasmine was grateful for this idea. 'Thanks, I will.'

'I'll make my drink while you're doing that. Take your time.'

Ten minutes later they were saying goodbye at the door. Jasmine went down the stairs with a spring in her step. She had enjoyed the evening with her friend, and was left with plenty to mull over. She felt a stirring of excitement about how her future might unfold, and about keeping in touch with Freya about her own plans.

In bed that night, Jasmine lay awake for quite a long time, her mind buzzing with everything that she and Freya had talked about, and more. And in ten days' time, she would be seeing Maider.

Chapter Six

A week passed by. Outwardly there was not much change. Work was just as interesting and stimulating, Mum and Dad were looking through property schedules, and the others were getting on with their school work. But Jasmine felt that there was a lot of change afoot inside her. Although she went over and over many of the same thoughts, she noticed that sometimes new ones would bubble up. Then some of those would disappear, but reappear later in a more solid version.

It might well be handy to live quite near to her work. Yet there was no way of knowing where she would be working by the time her family moved away. She loved her job at Snaith and Drew, but at this stage she had no idea what would happen once the agreed four months had passed. Living centrally would give good access to the largest range of work options, but her researches had quickly revealed that room rent was higher there.

Sometimes Jasmine's mind filled with ideas of moving away with her family. After all, by the time they went, her current post would surely be at an end. Such a plan was tempting, especially when she was feeling dejected about all the uncertainties in her future. Yet, however disheartened she could feel at times, there was a clear voice inside her that told her she should build her own independent life here, at least for now.

Her brothers were overtly grumpy with her for her determination to stay. She could find this hard, but always countered it by saying, 'It won't be all that long before you two are off somewhere, and you wouldn't give two hoots about how I felt about that if I were still at home!' They would acknowledge this with bad grace, and then revert to a low-grade occasional aside.

Uncomfortable though this was for Jasmine, she also found it helpful having to speak to them like this, as it kept in stark relief for her the knowledge that if she did not spread her wings, the others surely would, and she would still be at home when the twins and Poppy weren't there any more. And then home just wouldn't be the same. She loved Mum and Dad dearly, but what she loved most about home was the whole family being there.

Yes, now was definitely the time to take another step out into life – her own life. This didn't mean that she would be turning her back on her family. She could keep in close contact with them, and she could go and visit them. Mum and Dad had made it very clear from the outset that they were looking for a house that had enough room for them all. There might not be a room as large as the one she had here, but there would always be a bed for her, and the room could double as a guest room.

Soon it would be December, and the day that she was due to see Maider was the first of December. For quite a while Maider had lived in a cottage with her boyfriend, Tim, in a village about seven miles out of town, travelling by bus every day to the large insurance company where she worked. Jasmine had loved visiting her there, but recently she had moved into a place about half way between Jasmine's home and the offices of Snaith and Drew, and Jasmine had not yet seen it. She wasn't sure what had happened about Tim, but she imagined that she would hear all about that on Thursday. Apparently he worked abroad a lot. She had only met him once, and he had seemed nice enough. Jasmine was to go round to Maider's new place straight after finishing work, and they would spend the evening together.

When Thursday came, Jasmine learned that she was needed to stay on late at the office, so that meant she would not be leaving work until around six. She sent a text to Maider at lunchtime to let her know, and received a reply that said: No worries. Will look out for you after six. Mxx

Six fifteen saw Jasmine walking briskly along the route that she had chosen to get to Maider's. It was cold, and she could see her breath in the light from the street lights. She was glad of the walk. For some reason, she had felt that the heating in the office had been a bit oppressive that day. Some movement and fresh air was just what she needed. Another ten minutes, and she should be there.

As she turned the corner into Maider's street, she found that the roadside was crammed with cars, and that there were others coasting up and down looking for space to park. For a moment it looked rather odd, but then she realised that this road was just outside a metered zone. She checked the address on her mobile. Number 48: flat 4. That seemed straightforward enough. This end of the street was number 62, so she hadn't got far to go.

At first, number 48 appeared to be a brick-built detached house, with large windows of rooms on either side of the front door, and also on the floor above. She started to wonder if Maider had given her the wrong details. However, on closer inspection, she saw a sign pointing towards the rear of the house that said: Flats 3 and 4. She followed it and a light switched on automatically, revealing an external stairway leading up to a landing outside a door. She went up the stairs and was about to ring the bell, when the door flew open, and there was Maider.

'You made it!' She was clearly very pleased.

Jasmine gave her a hug. 'It's lovely to see you. Sorry I'm so late, but I did enjoy the walk here.'

'I put a stew on in the slow cooker,' Maider told her, 'so that I could be totally flexible about when you arrived.'

Maider was standing in a small lobby from which there were two doors. She opened one of them and invited her friend in, carefully securing the doors behind them.

Jasmine found herself standing in a pleasant hallway, the floor of which was polished wood.

'This is *really* nice,' she said.

'I like it a lot. I'm very happy here. Come and see my room.'

Jasmine followed her into a room of considerable size, where there was a bed, two comfortable chairs, a wardrobe, and a computer desk with an office chair.

'Wow! How did you find this place?' she asked.

'Actually, I heard of it through a friend of Tim's,' Maider explained. 'Look out of the window. You won't see all that much because it's dark, but you'll get some idea of how pleasant it is to look out over the garden ground.'

Jasmine put her nose almost on the glass and peered out. She could see that the next row of houses was two gardens away. 'How lovely!' she exclaimed.

'Apparently this house was split into four flats a long time ago. The current owners have reconnected the downstairs rooms, so that they have the use of both the ground floor flats. They have a young family – two little girls. There are two flats on this floor, and each of them houses two people. I share this one with a woman whose home is a couple of hours' drive away.'

'How odd,' Jasmine commented. 'Why would she want to be here?'

'She told me that she was made redundant a couple of years ago. She tried hard to find something near to where she lived, without success. Then she was offered something not far from here. I think she hasn't got many years before she's of retiring age, so I expect that's why she decided not to move. She's normally here from Monday to Friday. We get on fine together.'

Maider flopped down into one of the comfortable chairs, and Jasmine followed suit.

'Who's in the other upstairs flat?' Jasmine asked.

'It's two brothers. They seem to work very long hours, so I hardly ever see them. They always say hello, but that's about it.'

'So I gather it must be pretty quiet here.'

'It certainly is. That's why I don't mind paying a bit more than I'd planned to. After the peace of the cottage, I would have found it really hard to come to somewhere noisy.'

'I can understand that.' Jasmine paused for a moment, and then asked, 'Maider, do you want to tell me what happened with Tim?'

Maider's face went very pale, and Jasmine regretted having raised the matter. She wondered what to do.

Then Maider spoke through tightly-clenched teeth. 'He two-timed me.'

'Oh! I'm so sorry. Maybe I shouldn't have asked.'

'No, I'm glad you did.' Maider grimaced. 'I probably need to talk about it, but I've been avoiding it.'

'You could talk about it now,' Jasmine invited. 'The chat about flats can wait.'

Maider shook her head. 'No, that wouldn't be right. In any case, the Tim Betrayal story won't take all evening.'

'Okay,' Jasmine agreed. 'By the way, that time I met him he seemed an all right kind of person, but I suppose there can be things going on inside that don't always show themselves.'

'Too right,' agreed Maider. 'I met Tim not long after Mum and Dad were killed. At first we didn't see each other all that often, but when I finished at uni we started spending more time together. He was kind and reliable, and we got on really well. Gradually things progressed to the point where we decided to rent that lovely cottage and move in together. He got promotion at work, and although it meant a lot of travelling, we were both excited about it. We always kept in close contact whenever he was away... Well, at least I *thought* we did.' Here she pulled a wry face.

37

'How did you find out that there was someone else?' asked Jasmine.

'I knew nothing until he told me. I was completely blown away, especially as I'd never suspected anything.'

Jasmine was perched on the edge of her chair, leaning forward towards her friend. 'What did he say?' Her voice was almost a whisper.

'He told me he'd found someone else, and that he'd been seeing her for about six months. He packed up his things and left, saying that he would send me a cheque to cover his share of the rent for two months.'

'Didn't he tell you anything about who it was and where they had met?'

'No. And I'm glad he didn't because I don't want to know. All I know is that he two-timed me and that he isn't in my life any more.'

'And he said nothing about how it came about that he didn't want his life with you any more?'

'Nothing at all. Actually, I'd rather have it that way. I've heard some awful stories about departing partners saying horrible things as they leave. Tim didn't. He just gave me the information and left.'

'I wish you'd told me at the time,' said Jasmine sympathetically.

'So do I, but I couldn't speak about it. I could manage okay at work because all the conversation was about the job, but away from that environment, I was like an automaton.'

'It's so horrible!' exclaimed Jasmine angrily. 'He knew that you'd lost your parents suddenly, he led you to trust him, and then he went about things in a way that meant you lost him suddenly, too. No wonder you couldn't speak about it. You must have been in a state of complete shock.'

'Yes, I was, and actually I think I still am,' Maider confided. She looked stricken, and her eyes began to fill with tears.

Jasmine looked in her bag, found the small pack of

patterned tissues that she kept there, and handed it to Maider, who took it gratefully.

'Oh, aren't they lovely!' she exclaimed.

'Someone certainly had a good idea when they produced these,' said Jasmine. 'I chose the ones with autumn leaves on, but there was quite a range of other designs, too.'

'A lovely design on the necessary tissues feels like a wonderful thing.'

'You can keep that pack,' Jasmine told her, 'and then you'll know I'm thinking about you.'

'That's really kind. Yes, I'd like to hang on to the rest.' Maider tucked them down the side of the cushioned seat of the chair. 'That's me sorted out for now. Let's get on with the flat business.'

'Are you sure?'

Maider nodded emphatically.

Jasmine told her friend more about the imminent change in her circumstances. She had said a little on the phone, but now she explained everything that she knew so far.

'Ah, *now* I understand,' said Maider, 'and I think you're absolutely right to plan to stay around here.' She smiled. 'And I'm not saying that just so I can keep seeing you. By the way, one of the other things I really like about being here is the size of this room. The kitchen and bathroom are quite small, but that doesn't matter. Come and see.'

Maider led the way to the kitchen. On the way past the bathroom she opened the door for Jasmine to see inside. It was adequate in size, but only just.

The kitchen was similar. 'We usually take it in turns to cook,' Maider explained. She checked the stew. 'Looks well done to me. Shall we eat now?'

Jasmine nodded.

Maider handed a tray to her. 'I'll pile some things on it, and you can take it back to my room.'

When Jasmine took a mouthful of the stew, she was impressed. 'This is really good.'

'You must think that because you're hungry,' said Maider. 'It's nothing special really.'

Jasmine looked straight at her friend. 'Accept a compliment when you're given one,' she demanded playfully.

'Okay, okay, I will.'

'I've been wondering what it must be like living above the owners,' said Jasmine.

'It's fine with these people. They're really nice, and so are their children. We don't see much of each other, but I've had some interesting chats with them when I happen to encounter them. They've started up a veg patch in the garden, and I like watching the girls helping. They've offered me the use of a bit of ground at no extra cost, and I'm considering it. I said I'd tell them at Easter. I'd like to go ahead with it. The only problem would be if I wanted to go away for a while in the summer. There would be no one to water the plants if the weather was particularly dry.'

'Maybe I could pop round if I'm still in the area,' Jasmine offered.

'Oh, thanks.' Maider smiled. 'You could have some of the produce as a reward. Of course, we'd have to stagger our holidays.'

'We can keep in touch about it. I'll have finished my current job well before Easter, and by then I should have a much better idea about where I'm going to be living. I'm beginning to think that if I do go for a room in a flat, I'd like to be in a place where there's more going on. I can understand why you want somewhere quiet like this, but I'm so used to being in a family.'

'My advice is to keep on investigating – having a good look round, talking to people about flat life, and so on.'

'Thanks. I'm glad you think I'm on the right track. By the way, is there any news of your brother?'

Jasmine had never met Maider's half-brother, Stefan, but she had heard a bit about him. At thirty-five he was a lot older than Maider. His mother had died when he was very small, and when, years later, his father remarried, Maider was born.

'He's okay, thanks. We speak to each other on the phone from time to time. He and his partner, Clover, are thinking about having a child, but they haven't made a final decision yet.'

'Where's Clover from?'

'I think she's from Devon or Cornwall originally, but her parents moved out with her to Spain when she was quite young. They are still out there, and I believe that Stefan gets on well with them.'

Jasmine absorbed this information. 'That's good,' she commented. 'Do you think you might go out and see Stefan?' she added carefully. She knew that Maider had not been back to Spain since the death of her parents.

Maider stiffened, and hung her head slightly. 'Er... I might,' she said evasively.

'It sounds as if Clover and her parents are nice people,' Jasmine encouraged.

'That's just it,' Maider burst out. 'I might start crying while I'm there, and if I do, I don't think I'll be able to stop.'

'Maybe we could go together,' Jasmine suggested. 'I've never been to Spain. Hey, maybe I could go to some Spanish classes after Christmas...' Here her voice trailed off. 'But er... maybe I wouldn't manage very well.'

'Nonsense!' said Maider firmly. 'You can practise with me.'

'I'll see what I can find, then. And I can panic about my potential lack of linguistic skills while you panic about seeing your family.'

'Good idea!' Maider agreed. 'We could fly off in the summer and get someone else to water my veg plants.'

'It's great making plans,' said Jasmine. 'Let's see how many of them we can carry out! A lot of this is going to hinge on whether or not I can earn enough money for the

41

trip, but I'll certainly try.'

'If everything works out, I'd like to show you some sunflower fields,' Maider announced. 'Spanish sunflower fields are the only thing that I really miss. The colours are stupendous. Jasmine, it's really good talking like this. I shouldn't have put off a visit to Spain for so long. Staying here isn't going to bring Mum and Dad back.'

Chapter Seven

'I know your dad and I have been very preoccupied, but we've both noticed how quiet you've been,' said Jasmine's mother the following Saturday morning. 'I'm sorry I haven't been able to concentrate on your situation.'

'Don't worry, Mum,' Jasmine assured her. 'It's up to me to sort out my side of things.'

'Of course, and I don't want to interfere, but I do want to take my usual kind of interest. Are you still thinking along the lines of finding somewhere to live round here?'

'Yes, definitely. I've been looking at what's available, and when I saw Freya last week and Maider this week, I asked them a lot of questions. I found their answers really helpful, and I'm going to be in touch with them again soon.'

'Dad and I are only considering properties that have enough room for all of us.'

Jasmine hugged her mother tightly. 'I know that. I'm planning to come and visit, but I definitely want to live around here.'

'I'll miss you a lot,' said Mum. 'And it's no use pretending otherwise.'

'Me too,' Jasmine replied.

Over supper that evening, Dad made an announcement. 'Your mum and I have been thinking, talking and making plans.'

'What's new?' said Norrie rudely.

'Yeah, what's new,' Blake echoed, looking down at his plate.

Poppy was silent. She had managed to conceal the fact that Tippy was again curled up on her knee, hidden under the table – something that was forbidden – and that she was stroking him with her left hand while using her right hand for her fork. But she was just toying with her food and wasn't eating any of it.

Dad continued. 'I'll be moving into a rented room near my new workplace at the beginning of January.'

Norrie dropped his fork on to his plate with a loud crash.

'But I'll be home at weekends – Friday night to Sunday night.'

Here Jasmine spoke. 'When I saw Maider on Thursday, I found she was sharing a rented flat with a woman who had been made redundant a while ago and who had got a job near here. She's near retiring age, so she doesn't want to move house.'

'Sounds feasible,' said Dad. 'The thing is, I've still got plenty of years to go before retiring, so moving house is the best option. Your mum and I have a list of properties to view, and we'll be setting off very early on Monday morning. Norrie and Blake, we'll need you to be here for Poppy until we get back.'

'That's really boring…' drawled Norrie.

This time, Blake did not support him. Instead he stuck his fork into Norrie's ribs. 'Shut up!' he commanded. 'It's not easy for any of us, so just shut up.'

Norrie was so astonished that he made no further sound, except for the very quiet scraping of his fork on his plate.

'You can count on us, Dad,' said Blake. 'Poppy can come with us to school, and we'll meet up afterwards and come home together. You can be sure that Norrie and I will be in all evening, and you can ring us any time you want.'

'I could fix to go to a friend's house,' Poppy volunteered.

Mum looked at Dad. 'That might be the best solution,' she said.

Here Norrie intervened. 'No! It's our job. We'll be sixteen in March. We'll be the men of the house while

44

Dad's away.' He turned to Poppy. 'And I promise we'll do it properly. You'll see.'

'I could have taken a day off work if I'd known in advance,' said Jasmine.

'We thought of that, love,' Mum explained, 'but we didn't want to risk disrupting your job in any way when it's so important that you keep up a good profile.'

'That's where we come in,' Norrie told her. 'Blake and I are crucial participants in the project.'

'I'll keep my mobile switched on until the time when the three of you will be in school, and I'll do the same at three thirty,' Jasmine decided.

'That's great, but I can tell you now that you won't be needed,' Norrie promised.

'But you can do it anyway,' Blake acknowledged. He turned to Norrie. 'Can't she?'

Norrie nodded in the way he'd seen spies do in secret meetings on films. When this conversation began, he'd felt like a boy who was at the mercy of events beyond his control, but now he felt more in charge of his destiny... Well, of Poppy's at least.

'It might be quite late by the time we get back,' Dad warned them.

'You can be as late as you like,' Poppy informed them. 'My trusty bodyguards will see to it that Tippy and I are safe.'

The next morning, Jasmine was up promptly. Her brothers and sister were nowhere to be seen. Mum and Dad were busy making preparations for their early start on Monday.

'Can I have a look at the particulars for the houses?' Jasmine asked.

Mum turned to Dad. 'Have you printed them off yet?'

He shook his head, and then said to Jasmine, 'Have a look on my computer.'

Jasmine wasn't all that sure that she wanted to look at

45

them, as this would take her a step nearer to the reality of what the future would hold. Yet she knew in her heart that there was no way of avoiding the inevitable. The conversation she'd had with Maider had shown that up in stark relief. Poor Maider had been feeling that she wouldn't cope with her parents' death if she went to visit her brother, even though her parents had died years earlier. Jasmine could see that it was certainly best to keep abreast of things, however painful that might be.

In the event, she discovered to her surprise that she didn't find viewing the particulars painful at all. She soon became completely absorbed in studying floor plans and room sizes. In fact, she found the whole thing fascinating.

Although she knew that Snaith and Drew did quite a lot of conveyancing, this had never led to her looking at details of properties. She came to the conclusion that her interest was not solely in the house that Mum and Dad might decide to buy. Her mind had also stored details of the layout of Freya's and Maider's flats, and she was looking with a less uninformed eye than she would have applied only two weeks ago.

So absorbed was she that she did not notice the stealthy approach of her brothers until a head appeared over each of her shoulders. She jumped.

'What are you two up to!' she said crossly. 'You gave me a fright.'

They were both still in their pyjamas. Blake made an attempt to look like an evil monster, but it failed because he couldn't stop laughing.

'Let us have a look,' said Norrie.

Jasmine made room for them, and her brothers made a show of choosing the best bedrooms for themselves. However, they went on to do a search for details of secondary schools in the location of each property.

'We've got to help Poppy to get used to the idea, so that she'll settle in better when we move,' Blake informed

Jasmine seriously.

Jasmine said nothing, but inwardly she was impressed by the fact that her brothers were taking a more mature role so soon. And when Dad came through to print off the schedules, Norrie and Blake made him promise to text updates about how each house came across to him while on site.

Living through Monday was uneventful. It was a smooth operation, masterminded and conducted by Norrie and Blake, who did a superb job, including concocting some excellent food that evening.

Texts from the reconnaissance team – alias Mum and Dad – suggested that they had been drawn quite strongly to one particular house, and Dad had taken a lot of extra photos to show them all later.

Jasmine stayed in the kitchen after the others had gone to their rooms. She had said that she would do the tidying up, and it suited her to be alone for a while. There was a lot on her mind. Mum and Dad were certainly very keen on a particular house that they had seen, but surely they couldn't possibly follow this up yet. Perhaps they would put their home on the market straight away, but no one would know when it might sell. They must have some idea of how much they would get for it, or else they wouldn't know what price range to aim for when they were looking for a house. Maybe they'd already had someone round to value this house. She felt annoyed with herself that she hadn't asked them about that. But she had been preoccupied with her own researches, and they had been tied up with theirs. Now was the time when she needed to learn more about their situation and tell them more about hers.

What exactly was her own position? She had a full-time job that would last until the end of February, and she still did some waitressing at weekends. She had made a firm decision that she wasn't going to move away from here, but exactly how she was going to achieve this was not yet clear. Dad was going to be away a lot from the beginning of January, but many things would have to fall into place for her parents before they would have a date for the sale of their own house. Jasmine would have to find somewhere before the house was sold, but it made sense financially for her to stay on here meantime. The rather scary thing was that somehow she had to find full-time work, to start at the beginning of March.

Maider was paying more than she had originally planned for her place, but she had been in a full-time permanent post long before she had to look for somewhere on her own. Freya seemed to be content with the cost of her accommodation, but she, too, was sure of an income to finance it. It had been a good thing to talk to them, but Jasmine knew that her own situation was rather different from theirs, and she quickly came to the conclusion that she would have to look for somewhere quite modest, where the rent and bills were within the means of someone with a relatively low income. She imagined that there were places where she could share a room with someone. That would certainly work out cheaper, but the idea of sharing a room with a stranger didn't appeal to her at all. For one thing, she had been used to having her own room from when she was small, and for another, if she and the room-mate didn't get on, things would be very uncomfortable.

Maybe she could find something a little further out of town than she had first thought about, if that meant that the rent were less? And she could save on travel costs by walking.

Her thoughts were interrupted by the sound of the front door opening, and Mum and Dad came in. Although tired, they were animated.

Mum came straight to the kitchen.

'I'm glad you're still up,' she began. 'We've got such a lot to tell you.' She proceeded to give Jasmine a considerable amount of detail about where they had been and what they had seen.

Jasmine felt nonplussed. Mum was talking a bit like Poppy did when she was excited about something, and Jasmine wasn't used to seeing her like this. Her own thoughts had been interrupted, and besides, she needed to get to bed soon so that she would be fresh for work the next day. She realised that she wasn't taking in much of what Mum was saying, and she felt really uncomfortable.

Fortunately Dad joined them and took charge. 'I think we should leave the rest of this until tomorrow evening,' he said firmly.

'Yes, yes, of course,' Mum agreed hurriedly.

Jasmine took a deep breath. 'Yes, I need to get off to bed, but...'

'But what?' asked Dad.

'Er... there's something that's worrying me.'

Dad put his arm across her shoulders. 'Do you want to say a bit about it now, or can it wait until tomorrow?'

'When will this house go on the market?' Jasmine burst out. She clapped her hand to her mouth. 'Oh! I hadn't meant to ask quite like that. It's just that...'

'Don't think that you have to apologise,' said Dad swiftly. 'The fault is on our side. We should have kept you updated along the way.'

Here Mum took over. 'Jasmine, I think I've been pretending to myself that in the end you'd be coming with us, so I was always putting off the time when we would have to sit down with you and give you more details. I'm *so* sorry.'

'We had this house valued last week,' Dad told her. 'After that we narrowed down our choice of properties that we hoped to cover today. We think we might have struck lucky with the house we texted you about.'

'What do you mean?' asked Jasmine.

'In the present economic climate, it wouldn't be sensible

to try to push ahead with buying something until we had sold our own house, but in this case, it looks as if we might be able to get some kind of agreement about the new house before ours is sold.' He glanced at Mum, and Jasmine saw them smile at each other, as if sharing a special secret.

Dad continued. 'The owners aren't in a hurry to move. They're planning an adventure for themselves.'

All thoughts of going to bed had disappeared from Jasmine's mind. 'Did they tell you what it is?' she asked eagerly.

'They certainly gave us the broad picture,' Dad replied. 'They've bought a ruined croft on Shetland, and they're planning to do a lot of the rebuilding and repair themselves.'

'I got the impression that they'd inherited some money, and had decided to change their lives completely,' Mum added. 'They're going to get a caravan put there to live in while they're working on the place. They want to make a start around March time.'

Jasmine was grappling with the logistics. 'Even if the inheritance covered the cost of buying their property on Shetland, surely they'll need the money from the sale of their house to finance the cost of the caravan and all the materials for the work?'

Mum could not contain her excitement. 'They want to be sure that they've got a buyer for their house, but for all kinds of reasons they don't want to sell it yet. This fits our situation so well! Of course, there'll be details to be ironed out, but the big picture is looking good, really good.'

Jasmine felt herself being infected by her mother's emotions. 'I can hardly believe it!' she exclaimed. 'It all sounds too good to be true.'

'I know,' Dad agreed. 'We can't be certain yet, but the way things went today, there's a very good chance that it'll all work out. We're going to put our house on the market at the beginning of March. Ideally we'd hope to get a buyer who'll want to move in around the end of the summer, but we'll have to see what interest we get.'

Jasmine felt very relieved. This meant that she could live at home over the time when she was trying to get more work.

'Hearing all this is taking some of the stress off me,' she said. 'And now I feel really sleepy. Show me a few of the photos you took, and then I'll go to bed. No, on second thoughts, I'll wait until tomorrow, when the others can look at them, too.' She stood up, gave first Dad and then Mum a hug and a kiss, and then went upstairs.

The last thing she remembered before she fell asleep was of making a decision to start doing her Christmas shopping quite soon.

Tuesday evening was a happy time. The whole family sat round studying the particulars of the house that Mum and Dad had set their hearts on, and looking at the photos that they had taken. Poppy decided that Tippy would like the new kitchen, and then went on to argue good-naturedly with Norrie and Blake about who would have which bedroom. Mum and Dad didn't stop them. In fact, they joined in the fun.

The fascinating thing they all learned from Mum and Dad about the property was that it had originally been a police house. Apparently the current owners had bought it from the local council a long time ago, when it had been in a poor state of repair. There was a part that looked a little as if it had been converted from a garage, although there was no sign of a driveway to it. When Dad explained that it had been a police office and a cell, Norrie and Blake instantly seized on this, wanting it for their own private use. But Dad stood firm. A tasteful conversion of it to a sitting area with a fold-down bed and also a shower-room could be used by Jasmine whenever she visited, and by any guests, too.

Norrie and Blake could now be certain of staying on at their school for the rest of the academic year. They hadn't said anything of their concerns about what would happen, but Jasmine later overheard them muttering to each other about the relief that they wouldn't have to move while they were trying to get ready to take important exams. The way things were working out, when they started at a new school, it would be for sixth year. She knew that both of them wanted to go to university, but they seemed to be forever changing their minds about what they wanted to study.

Chapter Eight

The next time Jasmine saw Freya, she was keen to tell her all the news. She went round to her flat, where she met the new residents, who were two male foreign students. They seemed pleasant, and were keen to improve their English as quickly as they could. They did their best to try to persuade Jasmine and Freya to stay in and talk to them, but the young women had promised themselves another kind of conversation, and declined the persistent invitations.

Jasmine and Freya walked past the local pub, heading for another that they knew had some quiet corners in it. Seated with large glasses of orange juice and open sandwiches, they settled in for the evening.

Jasmine began by recounting the recent developments.

'That's great,' said Freya. 'It means that the pressure's off you for now.'

'Housing-wise that's true, but I'll have to keep an eye on the job market, of course. I do feel a huge sense of relief, though.'

'On completely another subject, I wanted to tell you that I got round to asking my mum how many times we moved before I was five.'

'What did she say?'

'Actually, I was blown away by what she told me. Apparently we moved every six months. I've got the information, but I don't think I've really taken it in yet.'

'I'm trying to imagine what that must have been like for you,' said Jasmine slowly, 'but it's really difficult to get my head round it. You would hardly have found your way round one house before you were off to the next. Did she say how far you moved each time?'

'Yes, apart from the first move, it was a long way.'

'So that means that when you moved none of the people would have been the same except for your mum and dad.'

'You're right! I hadn't thought about that.'

'It must have been pretty disturbing for you.'

'Oh, I don't know about that. I expect I got used to it quite quickly. After all, I didn't know any other way of life.'

'I can see what you're saying, but just think about it. Every six months you found yourself waking up in a different house or flat, in a different room, with a different view from the window, and different people walking around outside.'

'Mum did say she remembered that I was quite a clingy child,' Freya conceded.

'That doesn't surprise me at all,' said Jasmine. 'I remember when Poppy had to move nursery when she was nearly four. She insisted that we all had to go and see where it was. I realised it was because she wanted us all to know exactly where she would be, and I'm glad I went along with it. Norrie and Blake weren't very helpful about it, and Poppy got quite upset, so I bribed them with some new pens I'd bought with money I'd earned from my paper round.'

At this, Freya started giggling. 'That was very resourceful of you.'

Jasmine fell silent for a while, and Freya sipped meditatively from her glass of orange juice.

Then Jasmine continued. 'Supposing when you were between two and three we had lived next door to each other and played in each other's houses. Then supposing one day you moved away, a long way away, and we never saw each other again... It would be bad enough for me, having lost my friend, but at least I wouldn't have lost my house and all the other people who were around, whereas you would have.'

'Doesn't sound good,' Freya observed.

'No, it doesn't,' Jasmine agreed. 'And your mum and

54

dad *had* to keep moving because of your dad's job.'

'That's right.'

'Well, thank goodness for Gran, then,' said Jasmine. 'And on that subject, did your mum say anything about how much you saw Gran before you went to live with her?'

'No, she didn't, and I didn't think to ask her. I'll put that on my list for next time.' She stared at Jasmine. 'This feels sort of weird – as if it's the beginning of some kind of detective story.'

Here the conversation went on to a number of other subjects. Jasmine had discovered an unusual cookery book in a charity shop that she wanted to tell Freya about, and Freya wanted to talk about some new friends she'd met. She had managed to get one of her days off to coincide with an introductory session on making jewellery, and it had turned out to be excellent.

'When it came to the day, I nearly didn't go,' she admitted. 'I felt really tired, and as if I just wanted to potter around slowly, without any agenda. But when I got there, I found that I liked most of the other people, and I was very glad I'd turned up.'

'I expect they were mostly women.'

'Actually, about a third of them were men. I was quite surprised. And it was so interesting to see how their minds worked about what they wanted to make for themselves, and what they thought might look attractive on women.'

'Tell me more.'

'The person who led the class had brought along some samples of her work, and they were stunning! I couldn't wait to get started. She's so clever. In the morning she taught us some simple things to try, and they were very effective. Then, in the afternoon, she gave a talk on the range of materials that you can learn to use. Of course, some are very expensive, but there are plenty that don't cost much and look good.'

'That sounds great. Are you thinking of going on a

course?'

'It would probably be too difficult for me to get time off for a weekly class, but the woman said that if there was the demand, she would be willing to hold a day class once a month, or even consider providing a short course. If I knew about that far enough in advance, I might be tempted to use some of my annual leave.'

'I hope you do more of it. It sounds as if it could be your thing.'

'We've all got an open invitation to visit her at her studio. Of course, she said it would be best if we phoned in advance.'

'Sounds good,' Jasmine commented. 'Even if her main objective is to enhance her business, she's doing it by relating to people in a genuine way. I like the sound of that.'

'I get the feeling that there's a lot more to it,' said Freya. 'She comes across as having a real enthusiasm about people's ideas. It seems to me that she wants to help people to find their own creative skills.'

'That's the right way of teaching,' Jasmine reflected. 'What a difference there is between being forced to parrot what you're being told and being helped to discover things about a subject and about yourself in relation to it. So many teachers don't seem to realise this.'

'I know what you mean,' Freya agreed, 'but in a subject like nursing there's so much factual stuff that the only way is to drill it into the students, or get the students to drill it into themselves.'

Jasmine leaned forward towards Freya. 'But there's got to be some kind of balance,' she said earnestly. 'If I have a grasp of a subject from deep down inside me, I can make instinctive decisions from which I can act effectively.'

'I've found that in nursing there's not much room for instinct. There are so many protocols now, and if you don't stick to them you're in trouble.' Freya paused, and then added quietly, 'It's not too difficult to lose your job.'

Jasmine looked at her friend aghast. 'When you put it that way, I can see it. I think somewhere inside me I knew it was like that in modern medicine, but I hadn't really concentrated my mind on it. When I'm troubleshooting with computers, my gut instinct is invaluable, and anyone who turns to me for help is often looking for exactly that. Maybe your interest in making jewellery will give you something that you can experiment with.'

Freya laughed. 'Yes. The tutor is definitely one for being interested in what happens when you bend or ignore the rules!'

'Well, next year, not only am I going to have to look for more work, but also I'm going to end up not living with my family, and I'll need to find some other interests. So watch this space…'

'On the front of work, I wondered if you had ever thought of making a business out of your computing skills.'

Jasmine smiled. 'There's always been a family myth that Norrie and Blake and I would set up in business together, but I can't see it happening.'

'Why not?'

'They're still young, and I bet there are going to be some big surprises about the direction in which their lives take them,' said Jasmine wisely.

'You're sounding a bit like a parent rather than a sister,' Freya warned. 'Apply to yourself what you've just said, and you'll go in the right direction.'

Jasmine stared at her friend, then simply said, 'Thanks.' She glanced at her watch. 'It's nine thirty. Shall we stay until ten?'

'Sounds about right.' Freya looked away for a moment, and then said, 'There's something I wanted to tell you.'

'Go head.'

'It's about Gran.'

Jasmine nodded, and waited for Freya to begin.

'I've been thinking about her a lot since we last talked…

And I've been feeling guilty.'

'Guilty? What on earth for?'

Freya's eyes started to fill with tears. She tried to speak, but the words seemed to stick in her throat. She covered her face with her paper napkin.

Jasmine searched her mind for something to say. Freya's obvious struggle reminded her of times when she herself had been very upset. 'I'd like to help,' she said quietly.

Tears flowed down Freya's cheeks, and she managed to choke out, 'That's just it. You *are* helping.'

Jasmine was mystified. How could it be that she was helping, when it was all too obvious to her that Freya was becoming more and more upset?

'I'm sorry if I'm being a bit stupid, but I can't see how I can possibly be helping,' Jasmine murmured.

'Give me another couple of minutes, and I'll explain.' Freya's voice was muffled, but she sounded less distraught.

Jasmine still felt uncomfortable about her lack of useful input, and while she was wondering what her friend was going to say, she passed the time by taking very small sips of her drink.

When Freya emerged from behind the napkin, her face looked red and blotchy. 'I bet I don't look great,' she mumbled. 'I'll go to the Ladies and splash some cold water on my face. I won't be long.'

Jasmine nodded, and continued to sip at her drink.

Freya was back quite quickly, looking much better.

'Okay,' she began as she sat down, 'when you were so obviously astonished that I'd been feeling guilty, a whole torrent of feelings came rushing up from inside me. To be honest, I think they'd been squashed down and trapped there since soon after Gran died. Thanks for being a caring friend.'

Jasmine felt puzzled, but said nothing.

Freya went on. 'Do you remember me telling you what

58

Gran died of?'

'Yes, of course I do,' Jasmine replied. 'She had a massive stroke.'

'That's right, but I don't think I ever told you that it was me who found her, and when I did, she was still alive.'

Jasmine stared at her friend. 'No, you didn't tell me that. Have you been thinking that you could have saved her?'

'No. Well, not then.'

'What do you mean?'

'Jasmine, when I look back, I should have been able to see the signs.'

Jasmine leaned forward. She felt even more puzzled. All this was new to her, and it didn't make sense. 'What signs?'

'Over the months before that stroke, she'd had some funny turns. I should have done something about them.' Freya's eyes filled with tears again, and she grabbed her crumpled napkin.

'You once mentioned to me about your gran seeming a bit slow and wobbly one day, but you said she was fine again the following day.'

'Oh! I didn't remember I'd told you that. Well, it happened three times – about once a month. I should have insisted that she told her doctor what had happened. I did tell her I thought she should, but she just brushed that on one side. I should have phoned Mum, but I didn't want to worry her.'

'I wish you'd told me more. I would have got you to ring your mum. You shouldn't have been on your own with it all.'

Freya stared at her. 'You're right! I never thought of that. I shouldn't have been on my own with it.'

'It's a shame that your gran didn't see that. I expect she was so relieved that she got better each time that she didn't ever think about what it had been like for you to see her

59

struggling.'

'You know something... When I look back, I don't think she actually knew afterwards quite how unsteady she'd been.'

'She probably wanted to put it out of her mind.'

'Maybe, but perhaps she wasn't able to remember. Now I know quite a lot about the kind of things that can happen, I think that the funny turns she'd had were mini-strokes.'

'One of our neighbours had one of those,' said Jasmine. 'He was really wobbled by it, but he was fine the next day. He did eventually go to tell a doctor, who put him on something to thin his blood.'

'That's what should have happened with Gran,' replied Freya tearfully.

'Look, Freya,' said Jasmine firmly, 'you did your best. And when she had that big stroke you acted really quickly to get help, and you stayed with her, waiting for the ambulance to come.'

Freya looked unconvinced.

Jasmine tried again. 'I'm certain that if we could bring Gran back here and ask her, she'd leave us in no doubt at all that as far as she's concerned, you did everything, and more, than she could ever have expected.'

This seemed to get through to Freya. 'I take your point,' she acknowledged. 'There's just one more thing I need to say, and then I'd like us to talk about something else. I've realised that part of wanting to specialise in nursing elderly people is something to do with my guilt about Gran. Now that we've talked this evening, I know that I mustn't move job until I'm much clearer about things. I know I'll always enjoy chatting to older people, but that doesn't mean it has to be my main work.'

'Sounds right,' Jasmine agreed. 'Freya, I really like this place. Why don't we come here again?'

Freya smiled. 'I'd like to make a regular time, but with my shifts...'

'Don't worry about that, we can fix things up along the way. After all, you and I are only a text away from each other.'

'I feel I've swamped things with all my woes this evening,' said Freya ruefully.

'Well, I don't feel you have.' Jasmine kicked her friend's leg gently. 'And who knows, maybe next time *I'll* have something really pressing to talk about. For instance, Norrie and Blake have been threatening to buy a pet rat each, and if they go ahead...'

Chapter Nine

The run-up to Christmas was busy at work, and Jasmine was asked to do extra hours every week. Because of this she stayed on most days until six. Not only did she enjoy doing the extra work, but also she welcomed the increase in her income. She put it all into an online savings account that she had set up when she left uni. With all the fraud that was around nowadays, she was very glad that she was well aware of hazards and how to avoid them. There were times when she wondered how on earth much older people managed this. After all, when they were young, home computers hadn't even been thought about, let alone invented, and banks were secure establishments. She made a mental note to talk to Freya about this sometime.

The Christmas and New Year breaks were happy times. They were all aware that it would be the last Christmas they would spend there, and they decided to make it a really special one. Norrie, Blake and Poppy collaborated about the decorations, and Norrie and Blake surprised everyone by producing a Christmas pudding from a recipe from the days of the British Raj. When questioned about it, they remained secretive, refusing to reveal its source. Jasmine searched the internet, but could not find anything. Her brothers were becoming quite resourceful, and in unusual ways. Jasmine saw this as being very promising, and it was another step forward in her feeling that she no longer had any responsibility for them. She had a strange mixture of reactions to this. She had been so used to doing her share of keeping an eye on them that the change felt very unfamiliar and almost alien, and yet she welcomed being in a position where she could concentrate more on herself. The others weren't going to move away as soon as she had first thought, but January would bring with it the need for her to focus on her future employment.

There was certainly an option of using her IT skills as a business venture, but that would take time to arrange, and she felt uncomfortable about the prospect of needing to take money for something that she had always handed out freely and cheerfully. She began to wonder about speaking to a business advisor about such a project. Waitressing was something that she could always rely on. She had continued to do her regular weekend hours, and often received phone calls at short notice in case she could fill in on some weekday evenings. She had been inundated with requests over the festivities, and she had done her best not to turn any of that work down, but sometimes she simply couldn't fit it all in. And all the while, in her heart of hearts, she longed for further work at Snaith and Drew.

With everything that was on her mind, any thoughts of fixing up to attend a regular evening class in Spanish had faded away.

In the second week of January, Dad set off to spend his first few days familiarising himself with his new work setup. He had booked four nights at a B&B that from the details on its website looked quiet and homely.

It was after he had gone that Jasmine began to consider contacting the local Business Gateway to make an appointment to see an advisor. She felt uncertain about it, but persuaded herself that she was bound to learn something useful. She talked to several of her friends about it, and all of them encouraged her – particularly those who had benefited from her help with computing. In fact, all of them said that from now on they would expect to pay her for the advice they received from her, and that she must work out what she was going to charge.

One evening, she decided to go round and speak to a neighbour, Pete, whom she had helped in the past when he was setting up his home decorating business.

'You've got to take some of your own advice,' he stated abruptly, with a broad smile on his face.

Jasmine was bemused. 'What's that?'

'You seemed to have it all worked out when you were telling *me* what to do,' he reminded her.

'I'm a bit scared, and my mind's a blank,' Jasmine confessed.

'That's exactly what I said to you,' he told her triumphantly, 'only I was sweating as well.'

'Mm…' said Jasmine uncertainly. 'Now I wish I'd been a bit more empathic about how you felt.'

'I'm glad you weren't,' said Pete. 'It wouldn't have helped. What I needed was a plan, and the push to get on with it. You played a big part in that, and I remain immensely grateful to you.' He bowed theatrically. 'And now, I'll return the favour.'

Jasmine couldn't help smiling at the drama. 'Okay, I give in.'

'Giving in isn't a good start.' Pete took a pen and some paper from his desk and handed them to Jasmine. 'Get writing!' he commanded.

Playing for time, Jasmine wrote a heading: Business Gateway.

'Wrong!' Pete snapped, and Jasmine jumped. 'Try again,' he suggested kindly.

Jasmine groaned. 'I don't seem to be any good at this.'

'You've got it in you somewhere, because you were brilliant with me last year. Come on, girl, think!'

'It seems so obvious and straightforward when I'm doing it for someone else. I just don't understand this,' Jasmine mumbled.

'I'll give you a clue, then. How about a business name?'

Jasmine scribbled over Business Gateway, and wrote

Business Name instead. That felt better. Somehow she felt more herself.

'I'll need to brainstorm that,' she said briskly. 'I'll draw up some options over the next few days and then run them past you and some other friends.'

Pete nodded approvingly, and waited.

'I'll start thinking about what to put on a website, and when I've got my business name finalised, I'll get a domain name.'

Pete turned to a pile of invoices on his desk. 'I'll need to get on with these now, but come back next week and tell me where you've got up to.'

Jasmine left, her mind full of thoughts and questions, which she jotted down as she walked slowly back along the road. Aloud she announced, 'I won't see an advisor until I've got a shape round this.'

A week later she saw Pete coming back home in his van after work, and she flagged him down. He drew in at the kerb and ran the passenger window down.

'What's doing?' he asked.

Jasmine smiled. 'Plenty. I won't come round this week. I'll leave it until I'm further on with things, otherwise I'll feel I'm wasting your time.'

Although Jasmine appeared to be upbeat, Pete was not entirely convinced, and this showed on his face.

Jasmine grinned. 'I'm not slacking. Promise.'

'Okay, I believe you.' Sticking his hand high out of the driver's window, Pete waved as he drove off.

Dad's first week away had been a success, and Jasmine could tell that he was more relaxed than for a long time. Norrie and Blake always seemed either to be eating or to be in their room. As they were in the middle of taking their prelims, she imagined that they must be spending long hours studying. Poppy and Tippy were hardly ever seen apart, but they appeared to be very happy with one another's company, and Jasmine had heard Mum say to Dad that often Poppy had friends in to join her after school. Although Mum could be overheard muttering to herself about throwing out any old junk before they eventually moved, she was clearly savouring the prospect. Jasmine herself had always had a habit of paring down her possessions along the way, so her room was neat and was never overcrowded. The move would not require any extra sorting through of her things.

Dad had found that the B&B was fine for what he needed, but the owners of the place he and Mum hoped to buy had been in touch with a proposition. Their offer was to let Dad live in the converted police cell and keep an eye on the house and garden while they were away working on the property on Shetland. For this, they suggested a very low rent, together with payment for electricity. It didn't take Mum and Dad long to make their decision. A simple agreement was drawn up, and they and the other couple signed it. Dad would move in at the beginning of March.

Jasmine had been gradually advancing her business plans. The interest shown by her friends was an enormous help in the evolution of her thoughts on the subject. She was very glad of this, as her ongoing searches for local employment showed that things were pretty stagnant.

Then February came, and Mr Moran asked her to see him in his office at four thirty that afternoon. At first, Jasmine felt curious about this, and was looking forward to it, but as the day wore on, she began to feel rather nervous. She hadn't been aware of any problems with her work, but maybe there was something that she had done inadvertently that had caused trouble.

At four fifteen, she took a break, and sipped water unenthusiastically from a plastic cup. It was so important that she left this job with a good reference, and she didn't want anything to get in the way of that. The worst thing was that she couldn't think of anything she could do to prepare for this meeting. Each minute ground past as if it had lasted an hour.

Four thirty came at last. She knocked on Mr Moran's door and opened it.

Mr Moran looked up and smiled. She had always got on well with him, and she found this smile reassuring.

'Come in and sit down,' he said warmly.

Jasmine seated herself and waited to see what he would say. Although she felt better, her heart was beating rather uncomfortably, and she hoped that he would get to the point quickly.

'It's always seemed to me that you've been happy here,' he began.

'Very much so,' Jasmine replied.

'Unfortunately you have only another four weeks left,' Mr Moran pointed out.

'That's right.' Jasmine couldn't think of anything else to say that she thought would sound appropriate, so she fell silent.

Mr Moran went on. 'We will of course be delighted to provide a reference for any prospective employer. The work you have been doing here has been of a high standard, but we cannot extend your contract with us beyond the end of the month. However, I wanted to mention something in case it is of interest to you.'

Jasmine could hardly breathe as she waited.

'We are setting up a small satellite office in the village of Redchurch. It will open in the mornings from nine to one – the same as the local bank. We have budgeted for office support to cover two mornings a week, and wondered if you might consider applying for that post. We wanted to sound you out about this before drawing up a small advertisement.'

Jasmine felt in a quandary. She wanted a post, any post, with Snaith and Drew, but travelling to and from Redchurch would be relatively expensive, and she had no idea if the bus service would run at the times that she needed.

As if reading her thoughts, Mr Moran continued. 'We have someone lined up to see clients there three mornings a week, and we'll cover the other two mornings from this office. We could therefore offer you transport free of charge.'

'I'm certainly very interested,' Jasmine stated decisively, 'but can I take a couple of days to think it through, and then get back to you about it?' She took a breath and then asked, 'Do you have a start date yet?'

'The office will be open to clients from the beginning of April. The premises are currently being refurbished, and we hope to set up the office systems there during the latter half of March. I'll need to have your decision by next Monday. It occurs to me that it might be possible to modify your existing contract so that you remain our employee after the end of this month, although on reduced hours. I'll look into that and let you know later this week.'

'Thank you,' said Jasmine politely. Then she stood up and went back to the main office.

On the way home that day, Jasmine couldn't help occasionally skipping a step or two. She had been promised a good reference, and it looked as if the two mornings a week at Redchurch were hers if she wanted them. When she got back to the house, she felt like rushing up the drive shouting 'I've got some good news!' but instead she decided to keep it to herself. Yes, she wanted to make a decision about it *before* she told her family.

In bed that night, she wondered whether or not to mention anything to Mr Moran about her plans for her business. Perhaps she ought to tell him about any other employment. After all, right at the beginning she had done so. But maybe this was different. They weren't offering her full-time work, so surely it wasn't necessary to tell them how she intended to earn her living for the rest of her time. Then she suddenly realised that in a way she wanted Mr Moran's interest and approval. She pondered this. Could it be that with Dad away so much, she was looking for someone who would be like Dad always was until he had been made redundant? Before she went to sleep she promised herself that she would send a text to Dad, asking him to ring her the following evening.

Jasmine was surprised when Mr Moran approached her at the end of the next day, asking to speak to her again in his office. There he told her that if she decided to take the part-time post, her existing contract could be modified, and that she could start as soon as she had finished the remaining weeks of the current arrangement.

'That's great!' Jasmine burst out enthusiastically.

She regretted this instantly, as she wanted to sound poised and mature. However, Mr Moran was clearly pleased by her reaction.

'There's one more thing,' he added. 'The new post is at a level higher, and will attract an increase in your hourly rate.'

'I'll be in a position to give you my decision tomorrow,' said Jasmine confidently.

On her way home she checked her phone. Yes, there was a text from Dad to say that he would ring around eight.

That evening, the landline rang at ten to eight. Mum answered it, and when she realised that the call was for Jasmine, she immediately shouted up the stairs. Hoping that it was Dad, Jasmine was already on the landing, and she ran down to speak to him.

'I'm missing you,' she burst out.

'I'm missing you, too,' he replied sincerely. 'How are things?'

'I've been offered some very part-time work in a new offshoot of Snaith and Drew, starting at the beginning of March.' She didn't give her father time to respond, and rushed on. 'I'm going to take it, but there's something I wanted to ask you.'

'Can't you give me a minute to say "well done"?'

'Oh, thanks, but I want some advice.'

'Tell me what the problem is.'

'Over the past weeks I've been making plans to set up a small business – helping people with computing and IT. My friends have all been encouraging me, and I'm doing okay so far. My question is whether or not to tell Snaith and Drew about it.'

'Strictly, you don't need to tell them, but in your shoes I would,' Dad replied. 'They have experience of what you can do, and their knowing about your business might lead to other things.'

'Thanks, Dad, I hadn't thought of that angle,' Jasmine admitted.

'I'm so glad you got in touch, dear,' said her father affectionately. 'I want you to feel that I'm alongside you when you're taking steps forward in your working life. I've been so wrapped up in my own challenges over the last months that you might have felt I wasn't there for you.'

Jasmine relaxed. All feelings of needing Mr Moran's interest and approval for her business had evaporated, but she would certainly say something to him about it.

'Do you want to speak to Mum now?' she asked.

'Is there anything else we need to talk about first?'

'Not now,' Jasmine replied.

'Well, text me as soon as there is.'

'I certainly will.'

'In any case, let me know how it goes.'

'Okay,' said Jasmine happily. Then she called for her mother and handed the phone to her.

On the way to work the next morning, Jasmine wondered what would be the best time to speak to Mr Moran. However, that decision was taken out of her hands because he was already in work when she arrived, and he invited her into his office.

'I'll definitely take the post,' Jasmine told him, a little breathlessly. She hesitated only for a second before continuing. 'I also wanted to let you know that I'm in the process of setting up a small business, advising about computing and IT.'

'I'm very glad to hear that,' said Mr Moran. 'Your skills and knowledge have certainly been very valuable to us. I'll bear this news in mind.'

He said no more, but Jasmine had the distinct impression that he had something else he wanted to say. Feeling calm, she settled down to her work of the day.

She didn't have to wait long to discover what was on Mr Moran's mind. After lunch, he handed her an envelope.

'This is a formal request that you let us have your business details, so that we can contact you for sessional work at this office.' He went on to explain that before she had worked for them, they had employed IT support from a specialist firm, but that this had not been necessary during her time there.

Jasmine felt as if her whole body was glowing, and that her feet were no longer quite touching the ground. She longed to send a text to Dad straight away, but she would have to wait until she was on her way home. The letter felt like a wonderful prize, and she tucked it safely in the broad pocket of her handbag.

Hurrying home at the end of the day, Jasmine was only barely aware of the biting wind. Thus far, it had been a relatively mild winter, without any signs of snow, but now there was sleet in the air. First she sent a text to Dad, and then she went to Pete's house, but his van wasn't there. Never mind, she could tell him about her triumph later.

At home she waited until Dad's call before she opened the letter. She read it out to him.

'Excellent!' said Dad. 'It looks as if your first client is already in the queue.'

'It's a bit scary, but in a nice sort of way,' Jasmine confided.

'I know the kind of feeling,' Dad told her. 'I remember having it when I was your age, and actually I'm getting a bit of it now with the opportunities that are around me.'

'Let's hope that things go well for both of us, then.'

'I think the future could be very interesting,' Dad replied. 'We've just got to keep our eyes open, and keep pushing forward where and when we can.'

Jasmine made a mental note to write down these wise words as soon as she went off the phone. And she decided that she must have another chat with Freya soon, as she wanted to get her reaction to her thoughts about helping older people with home computing.

Aloud she said, 'I'll go and get Mum. She was saying something about needing to talk to you.'

Chapter Ten

Jasmine and Freya were once more seated in their favourite corner at what was now their preferred pub. On the table in front of them were large glasses of apple juice and two plates of bean salad, piled high.

'Where shall we begin?' asked Jasmine. 'Salad or chat?'

'Salad for me,' Freya replied. 'I'm starving.' She took a long drink from her glass, and began to eat from the substantial serving of beans.

'Hey, you'd better chew that before you swallow it,' warned Jasmine. 'You're behaving as if you haven't eaten anything for a week.'

'I certainly feel as if I haven't,' Freya managed to say through a large mouthful. She swallowed, almost painfully, and added, 'I've been rushing around all day, and breakfast was a very long time ago.'

Jasmine laughed. 'I get the picture. Look, I can wait a bit before I start my food. How about I talk while you're eating, and then you can take over while I'm eating.'

Freya nodded enthusiastically.

'Okay, off I go.' Jasmine went on to tell her friend about the developments at Snaith and Drew.

'Sounds good,' Freya commented briefly while plunging her fork into her food.

Jasmine then went on to tell her about her business plans and the hope of extra work from Snaith and Drew.

'But what I'm keen to talk through with you this evening are my ideas about home tuition for computer use for older people.'

Freya was now down to the last layer of salad, and was

eating at a more normal rate. 'Go ahead, I'm nearly ready to speak.'

'The more I think about it, the more I can imagine that there are a lot of older people who don't go out much, and would like to be able to use a computer, or maybe need to learn more about what they can do with the one they've got.'

'Or need someone to come round when something goes wrong with their computer,' Freya finished for her. 'How often have I heard about people panicking when their internet connection isn't working, or an electronic file has gone missing. And it's not just people in their seventies and eighties, you know, it's people in their fifties upwards. Frankly, I think that if people got to know about you, you'd be inundated with requests for help.' Freya popped another forkful of food into her mouth.

'Oh, I wouldn't like to be overloaded,' said Jasmine quickly. 'I'd feel guilty if I couldn't get round everyone.'

'Well, that's something you're going to have to think about. And what are you going to charge? You'll have to earn enough to keep yourself, and if you're going to people's homes, you've got to take into account the fact that you'll be spending time travelling – time that you won't be getting paid for.'

'I know. I've been thinking about those things, and more, but I haven't come to any conclusions yet. That's why I wanted to talk to you.' She paused for a moment before continuing. 'Maybe I could offer some low-price introductory sessions – one per household – then see what I learn from that exercise, and go forward from there.'

'That's not a bad idea,' Freya approved.

'I expect that people who are at home a lot might prefer a daytime visit.'

'Very likely.'

'I could do Saturday mornings until I finish my full-time job,' Jasmine mused. 'And of course, I'll offer discounted rates for people on low incomes.'

'I think your biggest problem is likely to be making sure that you end up with enough money for yourself,' Freya pointed out carefully. 'It's all very well wanting to help people and making your services affordable for everyone, but if that means you're starving in a garret, you won't be any use to anyone.'

'I wish I didn't have to think about all that,' Jasmine replied. She fell silent. Then she said briskly, 'Right. I must get to grips with it.'

Freya smiled across at her.

Jasmine smiled back, and noticing that her friend had very little left on her plate, she asked, 'Have you got any more information about Gran yet?'

'As a matter of fact, I spoke to Mum a couple of nights ago. She told me that when I was little, I used to see Gran quite a lot because when Dad was away, Mum often used to come across here with me and stay for a few weeks. That went on even after I'd started school, although then she couldn't do it as often. She had to wait for times when it was school holidays and Dad was away at the same time. It's funny how I don't seem to remember it.'

'Perhaps those memories are all wrapped up together with living with Gran during term time,' Jasmine suggested.

'I suppose they could be,' Freya agreed. Then she froze.

'What is it?' asked Jasmine.

'I've just seen someone come in that I don't want to have anything to do with,' Freya whispered.

'What do you want to do?'

'Come to the toilets with me,' said Freya desperately. 'And don't look round.'

Jasmine did as her friend had asked, and soon they reached their haven. Fortunately, they were alone.

'What is it?' Jasmine repeated.

'There aren't many horrible people at work, but one of them just came in. His name is Mick, and he thinks he's every woman's idea of the perfect man. I can't stand him. If

75

he'd seen me, he would have come and joined us, and then I'd have been stuck with him. He always comes across as being so personable, but underneath he's not someone you'd want to have anything at all to do with. Believe me, I know. I would have had to watch him chatting you up, and I promise you, you would have fallen for his fake charms.'

Jasmine was shocked. How awful. She felt fortunate that she had never had to deal with this kind of thing before. There had been some sticky moments on a few of the nights out at uni, but with a bit of ingenuity, she'd never found herself embroiled in anything really unpleasant.

'We'd better leave,' she decided.

'That's a forgone conclusion. It's how we go about it that's the problem,' said Freya.

Just then, the door opened and a middle-aged woman came in and stood in front of one of the mirrors. Freya began to talk animatedly about one of her favourite songs. The woman re-did her lipstick, and then left.

'We've already paid for the food and drinks,' Freya reminded herself. She looked straight at Jasmine. 'We've got to get out. Will you do me a huge favour?'

'If I can.'

'Will you link arms with me, and we'll walk out together like that?'

'Of course, but I'd better go and grab our coats first. What does he look like?'

'You can't miss him. He's wearing a dark purple shirt with a weird black motif on the left of his chest.'

Jasmine left Freya, and walked confidently across to pick up their coats. As she returned to the toilets, she glimpsed a man in a dark purple shirt standing at the bar with a woman who was dressed quite provocatively.

'It's okay,' she told Freya. 'He's busy. Put your coat on, and we'll go.'

Arm-in-arm, and smiling at each other, Jasmine and Freya crossed briskly to the exit door. Then they were out in the street, and Freya was taking in large gulps of cold fresh air.

'Come up to the flat for some calming tea?' she suggested.

Jasmine checked the time on her mobile. 'Okay, but I mustn't stay long.'

Back at the flat, the foreign students were pleased to see them, but Freya was barely civil. In the peace of her room, she flung herself down on her bed.

'Sorry, but I don't think I can ever go back there again,' she stated. Then she shuddered. 'He makes my skin creep.'

'I'm sure we can find somewhere else,' said Jasmine cheerfully. 'He can't be in more than one place at a time.'

'Curiously, it can feel as if he can. But you're right, and there are plenty of good places to choose from.'

On the way home that evening, Jasmine reflected on what had taken place. She had been surprised by the intensity of Freya's reaction, but she did not doubt that there was good reason for it. Freya hadn't offered any specific stories, and Jasmine hadn't wanted to ask for any. It was enough to accept that this was definitely someone to be avoided.

Chapter Eleven

March came, and Dad moved into the police cell. Norrie and Blake couldn't stop making jokes about this, and Jasmine sometimes overheard them rehearsing together before trying out the next one.

She found that changing to the new work routine was not as challenging as she had feared. She was still based at the main office for the first two weeks of her reduced hours. After that she would have to arrive there twenty minutes early in order to get her lift to Redchurch. The new office was in what had been the post office until it was transferred to a counter at the back of the local supermarket. She quickly applied herself to setting up the computer and filing systems, ready for the early April opening.

Her efforts to arrange other employment had born fruit, and although her total income would be reduced significantly, she would have enough to cover things while she was still living at home. She had been given extra waitressing hours at the restaurant on a regular basis, with a promise of this continuing for the foreseeable future. A friend of Pete's had approached her for help. The friend's wife had been unwell for several months, and the paperwork for his plumbing business had got into a terrible mess. He begged Jasmine to do everything she could to make sense of the confusion. Jasmine was all too happy to oblige. She asked him to bring it all round, and she spent many hours going through it in her room whenever she had time.

In addition to all of this, Jasmine had drawn up some flyers advertising introductory sessions of home computing, and had bravely put them through the doors on streets where she knew that there were a lot of older people. This had produced some phone enquiries, and already she had four people booked in, with another two promising to get back to her later. She began to wonder if there might be a demand for small classes of three or four people at time, but as she had no base from where she could hold sessions, she decided not to offer this yet. However, the idea lingered on in her mind. It would certainly reduce the costs for clients, and perhaps in between lessons they might help one another.

She had written down some ideas of what to call her business, but the more she thought about it all, the more she decided to wait and see how things developed. Because her original ideas of earning an income had already expanded into some other areas, she thought that she would include some of those services on her website as well. Maybe the business name needed to be less specific than she had originally thought.

On the website she would display a good photo of herself, together with her qualifications. She would list the services that she could offer, and an hourly rate for each. And whenever she gained experience with customers who showed satisfaction, she could display feedback. For contacting her, she could have an e-mail address and her mobile phone number.

Yes, it would definitely be better to gather more ideas, information and experience before she finalised a business name and obtained a domain name. The only problem had been what to say to Snaith and Drew about the fact that her business details were as yet incomplete. She spoke to Mr Moran about this. The conversation was very helpful, as it led to her setting up a business account at the local bank – account name: Jasmine Simmons t/a Office Support Services. This meant that clients like Snaith and Drew could pay directly into that account. It was all very exciting, especially as she had heard that they wanted to book some of her time as a specialist advisor in the second half of April.

'Specialist advisor': Jasmine turned this term over in her

mind. It sounded very good, although a bit grand. However, when she told Dad, he pointed out that it simply described a service that she was well able to offer, and she could see what he meant.

There was now so much for Jasmine to think about, arrange, and advance, that she was less aware of what was going on at home, so that when early one evening she encountered some strangers on the landing she had quite a shock. Fortunately she managed to suppress an impulse to ask them what they were doing there, and before she had worked out what to do instead, Mum came up the stairs.

'I'm just showing Mr and Mrs Howells round, dear,' she said in slightly stilted tones.

'Oh... er... of course,' Jasmine replied. She managed to smile at the intruders, and added politely, 'I'm working on some invoices this evening. I'll leave the door open so that you can come and look at the room whenever you're ready.'

Inside the temporary safety of her room, she grimaced and murmured, 'That was a close one.'

Then she heard the door of Norrie and Blake's room opening, and the sound of Mum's voice. 'And this is another double bedroom.'

To Jasmine's utter astonishment she heard her brothers say 'Good evening.' Yes, it was definitely their voices, but the words and tone were completely alien to their habitual way of presenting themselves.

Next, the Howells came into her room. 'We're sorry to interrupt you,' said Mrs Howells.

'Not at all,' Jasmine replied. 'I'll have to pop downstairs for a minute to get something. Please do take your time.'

In the kitchen, Jasmine discovered that Poppy had found some boxes of tea bags, had laid out some of the best cups and saucers on the kitchen table, and had boiled the kettle. Tippy was nowhere to be seen.

'Where's Tippy?' Jasmine asked her in a low voice.

'I put him in the shed in his carrying cage with some nice treats to keep him quiet. I couldn't risk him jumping on the table and spoiling everything,' said Poppy earnestly.

Jasmine stifled the laughter that rushed up inside her. 'Good thinking,' she replied.

It wasn't long before they heard footsteps on the stairs, and Mum saying, 'Would you like a cup of tea?'

'That's very kind of you.' Mr Howells spoke rather formally.

'Thank you,' said Mrs Howells. 'It would certainly give us time to think of any other questions we want to ask.'

Poppy switched the kettle on again, and smiled very sweetly as the Howells appeared in the kitchen. 'What kind of tea would you like?' she asked. 'I have three different kinds here.'

Mrs Howells was clearly impressed, and she gave her husband a meaningful glance before saying, 'That blackberry infusion looks very nice.'

Poppy washed her hands and then carefully took two of the blackberry teabags from their box, dropping one into each of two china cups, and then pouring boiling water on them.

'Would you like a cup as well, Mum?' she asked.

'Thanks. I think I'll have some ginger and lemon,' Mum replied. Then she turned to the Howells. 'I'm sorry that my husband can't be here this evening. He won't be back until late.'

Jasmine felt rather puzzled by this latter statement. Today was Thursday, and Dad wasn't due back until tomorrow evening. She turned to her sister.

'Poppy, could you give me a hand upstairs with something?'

Poppy quickly understood the message, and they left the kitchen together, closing the door behind them.

As they entered Jasmine's room, they found Norrie and Blake sitting side-by-side on her bed.

Poppy had been looking forward to a private chat with Jasmine. 'What are you doing here?' she demanded.

'We need a confab,' Norrie and Blake replied together.

'I don't think we do,' Jasmine said firmly. 'What we need to do is keep really quiet.'

'Why?' asked Poppy, who liked the idea of a sibling meeting.

'I think you've forgotten that my room's directly above the kitchen,' Jasmine whispered.

Poppy clapped her hands to her mouth, saying, 'Oh no!' between her fingers.

'You two can come into ours,' said Blake.

Quietly they all moved into the brothers' room.

Norrie began. 'We don't like strangers rooting through our house.'

Jasmine was about to say something sensible, but Blake got in first. 'It's all very well moving to another house and going to another school. It might even be exciting. But it's really bad having people nosing around here.'

'We've just got to put up with it because we've got to sell this house,' said Poppy reasonably.

Jasmine said nothing. Poppy was being very grown up and she wanted to let her enjoy the experience.

'I only hope that that lot buy it,' Norrie stated crossly. 'Then the rooting will stop.'

Poppy didn't know what to say to this, and she turned to Jasmine.

'The truth of the matter is that we might be lucky and sell the house to some of the first few people who come to view it,' said Jasmine, 'but we've got to be ready for this to go on and on – for months if necessary.'

Blake threw up his hands in mock horror. 'You mean a perpetual invasion?'

Norrie groaned. 'It won't seem like our home any more.'

Silently they all stared at one another.

Then Jasmine said, 'We all know that it won't be long before it isn't our home, and however much we like the next house, we'll miss this one.'

'Too right,' Blake acknowledged. His voice sounded a bit muffled, and he went off to the bathroom for a few minutes.

Eventually, the sound of the front door closing allowed the 'confab' to disband. Poppy raced downstairs to talk to Mum about the event, Jasmine returned to her paperwork, and Norrie and Blake grumpily banged their door shut.

When Jasmine later looked up and glanced out of her bedroom window, she could just see in the gloom the shape of Poppy opening the shed door to release the imprisoned Tippy. She felt that she could understand why Mum had lied about the day of Dad's return. The Howells appeared to be entirely genuine, but you could never be completely certain in a situation like this.

Before Jasmine went to bed, she spent some time discussing the viewing with her mother.

'They seemed interested, but they had other properties to look at,' Mum began.

'Do you know where they're from?' asked Jasmine.

'Northampton. They didn't say anything about why they were moving.'

'They looked a bit older than you and Dad. Did they mention anything about children?'

'They've got a daughter who lives about half an hour's drive away.'

'I wonder why they're looking at a house this size?'

'There's no way of telling.' Mum sighed. 'Oh well, that's the first viewing, and it might well be one of many.'

'We were talking about that upstairs,' said Jasmine.

'It could get pretty wearisome keeping everything extra-tidy, and for I-don't-know-how-long.'

'We've just got to look at it as another phase in our

lives,' said Jasmine wisely.

'Yes,' Mum agreed. 'That's the only way forward.'

When Jasmine climbed rather wearily back up the stairs to go to bed, she realised that in her heart of hearts she hoped that her family would not move away until it was nearly the start of the schools' autumn term. That would be the latest time they could move without disrupting her sister's and brothers' education. Jasmine felt that she needed time to build up her business, and then work out what kind of accommodation she could afford.

Jasmine usually slept well, but that night she was quite restless. She was aware of dreaming of unfamiliar rooms, in houses that meant nothing to her. At times she felt that she wanted something to eat, but she wasn't hungry, and in any case she was too tired to go downstairs to the kitchen. As the night wore on, she began to feel pain in her abdomen, and she worried that she might be sickening for something.

The next morning Jasmine was quite relieved when the alarm on her mobile phone brought her to full consciousness. She had been dozing, but didn't feel comfortable. She got up straight away, and went to have a shower before the others were up. She felt quite agitated, but found that the warm water calmed her a little.

The idea of breakfast did not appeal to her, and instead she sipped from a cup of hot water as she packed a couple of slices of bread in her handbag. Although Friday wasn't one of her usual mornings at Snaith and Drew, they had contacted her to see if she could cover at the main office, as someone had a hospital appointment. She could hear the others stirring. Unusually for her, she felt that she didn't want to see them, so she left the house early. Thank goodness Dad would be home this evening. Although she wanted to get on with the plumber's paperwork, she hoped to spend some time with Dad over the weekend. She didn't know quite what she wanted, but she had a feeling of urgency about needing contact with him. On the way to work, she even considered ringing him, but decided against it. She needed him to be there in person, and not as a presence at a distance.

She had nearly arrived at Snaith and Drew when fear gripped her. Almost immediately the grumbling pain in her abdomen increased, and she clutched at herself. Jasmine was ill only rarely, and these symptoms alarmed her. What could this be?

When she went into the office, there was no one around and she went straight to the toilets, hoping to be able to gather herself, ready for the day. She splashed cold water on her face, and looked in the mirror. She certainly looked pale, but tried to tell herself that this was only because of not sleeping well. Then her mind flooded with another fear. What would happen to her if she had an illness that meant she couldn't work? She had never before considered what self-employed people did if they were off sick for a long time. Maybe this is what she needed to talk to Dad about... Her stomach contracted uncomfortably, and for a few moments she felt quite sick, but after that the pain cleared, and she felt that she could face the day.

She was busy with her first task when Megan Cowan arrived. It was exactly nine o'clock.

'Hello, Jasmine. Busy already? I knew we could rely on you,' she commented cheerfully as she hung up her coat.

Jasmine looked up and smiled. She liked the secretary, and had always got on well with her.

'You're looking a bit peaky this morning,' Megan observed.

'I didn't sleep all that well,' Jasmine told her, 'but I'll be fine.'

'Yes, you can catch up at the weekend.'

They both fell silent as they concentrated on their tasks. The phone rang, and Megan answered it, but Jasmine had no idea what it was about, as her focus was entirely on her work and also on her future.

Chapter Twelve

Jasmine had stayed up until Dad arrived home, and it was rather late by the time she went upstairs. She had no doubt that she would sleep like a log, but instead she found that this was like the previous night – full of disturbed tossing and turning, and those stabbing abdominal pains were back with a vengeance.

Eventually she fell into a deep sleep, and didn't wake until after ten o'clock. She felt quite disorientated, particularly as the last time she had looked at the clock it had been around five thirty. Well, there was one good thing. Dad had suggested last night that they went out for lunch together – just the two of them – so she didn't have long to wait before she could discuss some of her worries with him.

Downstairs she found Mum tidying up in the kitchen, but the others were nowhere to be seen.

'Where is everyone?' she asked.

'Oh, they're somewhere around,' said Mum vaguely.

Jasmine thought that she looked quite distracted, and assumed that she had a lot on her mind. She wandered into the sitting room, where, to her surprise, she found Dad sitting in the middle of the sofa with Poppy on his knee, and Norrie and Blake sitting up close on either side of him. They were all watching what looked like a very silly cartoon, with the sound turned off. The other thing Jasmine noticed straight away was that they were all still in their night clothes. She couldn't help chuckling at this sight, and her anxieties seemed to disappear in a flash.

Three heads swivelled round and scowled at her. 'It's not funny!' Poppy stated emphatically, wrapping an arm round Dad's neck.

'Not so tight, love,' Dad told her gently. 'I need to breathe.'

'We're off to get dressed,' said Norrie and Blake together.

'Can I join you?' Jasmine asked Poppy kindly.

'No! Well, you can for a bit,' Poppy added begrudgingly. 'Dad said he's going out with you for lunch, so he's mine for now.'

Jasmine noticed that Tippy had appeared outside the window and had started yowling mournfully. 'I'd better go and let him in,' she said.

Poppy surprised her by saying, 'Well, don't let him in *here*.' She clutched at Dad's neck again, and Jasmine saw that he had to ease her arm away from his windpipe.

'Okay, I'll give him something in the kitchen,' Jasmine replied cheerfully.

A couple of hours later, Poppy was back to her usual self, and was happy to wave goodbye to Jasmine and Dad as they walked off in the direction of the local garden centre for their lunch. Norrie and Blake were nowhere to be seen.

On the way along the road, Dad informed Jasmine that he was going to do something with her brothers that evening, although it hadn't yet been decided what that would be. It seemed to Jasmine as if each of her siblings in their own way had been struggling with not having their usual contact with Dad. And now, she felt a lot more confident about her impending chat with Dad.

Seated in the large heated conservatory which served as a pleasant eating place, Jasmine and her father each had a large baked potato in front of them, the fillings of which spilled out across their plates. Jasmine first asked her father how he was finding his new job and his temporary home in the police cell.

'The job's so interesting,' he began enthusiastically. 'More and more I can see opportunities for expansion. I get on well with my bosses and all the other staff. As you're probably only too aware, my redundancy came as a terrible shock, but that black cloud is certainly turning out to have a silver lining.'

Jasmine smiled. She was so pleased for her dad, and it was also a weight off her mind to learn that he was settling in so well.

Dad went on. 'And the police cell is really cosy. I'm sure you'll love it when you sleep there.' He hesitated for a moment before adding, 'Jasmine, are you *sure* you don't want to move with us?'

Jasmine nodded emphatically. 'Yes, I'm certain,' she confirmed. She thought she saw a look of disappointment flash across her father's face, but she couldn't be sure, so she decided not to say anything about it.

'I don't like the thought of leaving you behind, but I do know that at twenty-three you're more than ready to be branching out.'

Jasmine felt touched by her dad's obvious sadness at the thought of her leaving the family, and she felt supported by his recognition of her actual situation. She took a small mouthful of potato, and finding that the horrible abdominal pains were entirely absent, she enjoyed it. She hadn't eaten much yesterday and had missed breakfast this morning, and she realised that she was pretty hungry.

After they had both eaten in silence for a while, Jasmine decided to make a start.

'Dad, I think I've been doing really well so far in building up my self-employment, but I've got some worries I wanted to run past you.'

'Fire away.'

Jasmine felt tears pricking in her eyes. She wanted to discuss all of this in a mature way, but at the moment she felt a bit like a child.

She took a deep breath. 'I've set myself a target of the beginning of September. By then I've got to have built up

my income enough to be able to pay for a place in a flat.'
Jasmine paused, and then pressed on. 'But I realise that I've
started to panic in case I don't meet that target, particularly if
I get ill or something.'

Dad looked at her with obvious sympathy in his eyes.
'I've had quite a lot of friends over the years who've been
self-employed,' he told her. 'As they've built things up,
they've eventually taken out insurance for if they can't work
for a while because of illness. I do know that it could be a
worrying time in the early stages, before they've been in a
position to do that.

'Jasmine, you're a hard worker, and you deserve
success. I want to help you in whatever way I can. Your
mum and I are in an uncertain time financially, although
things do seem to be pulling round now. We're moving to
an area where the housing is a bit cheaper than around here.
If everything works out about the sale of our house and the
purchase of the police cell house, we should end up with
some spare capital. And we do have some savings. I'll have
a word with your mum, and I'm sure she'll agree that we can
be a financial catching net for you if necessary over the next
year or so. In any case, you'll need a deposit when you get
your room in a flat, and we can give you the money for that.'

Jasmine's face flushed. She felt embarrassed that she
hadn't yet thought about the issue of a deposit, and she was
glad that it had been raised in the privacy of this
conversation.

'Are you sure?' she asked. 'I don't want to put any
stress on you and Mum.'

'Of course I am,' Dad assured her.

'Thank you so much. I'll keep you updated along the
way with where I'm up to with my earnings, and what plans
I'm making to expand my activities.'

'That won't be necessary,' Dad told her gently.

Jasmine drew herself up. 'Well *I* think it is! After all, in
effect you're making a kind of investment, and so you need

to have information about how that investment is progressing,' she stated in a very business-like way.

'That's well thought out, Jazz!' Dad used the name he'd sometimes called her when she was young.

'Anyway, the discipline of drawing up those updates will be of benefit to me,' Jasmine added. 'I'll have a clear idea of exactly where I'm at. I think I'll do it fortnightly to begin with, and see how it goes.'

'Monthly would probably be sufficient,' Dad commented.

Jasmine shook her head. 'No, not at first, anyway. Maybe later.'

'I always knew that I had a very clear-headed daughter, but it's great to see you in action like this.'

Their food finished, they stayed on for a while, relaxing together, before finally walking back to the house. As they strolled along, Dad remarked on how the air had a hint of spring in it, and how he liked the increase in daylight hours.

Chapter Thirteen

When Jasmine handed over her completed work to Pete's plumber friend, it was very gratefully received. Straight away he paid her the sum that they had originally agreed. Later he handed in an envelope containing a twenty-pound note and a card, inside which his wife had written that now everything was sorted out and so well organised, she felt that she could take over most of the work again without fear of becoming overwhelmed by it.

Jasmine felt a warm glow inside as she read this. The outcome of her efforts was exactly what she had hoped. Then she read the rest of what was written in the card. It went on to say that Jasmine could use this as a testimonial, and that she would let her friends know what a good job Jasmine had done. Jasmine put the card on a shelf near her bed, and hugged herself. She had enjoyed doing that assignment.

That evening, she sat up late, devising a set of weekly planners. She had her engagements diary and prompts on her phone, but she wanted something else as well. A fair-sized chart for each week could show her engagements, but would also allow plenty of space for pencilling in ideas and suggestions. Tomorrow she would go and buy a large pin board, on which she would display a month's worth of charts at a time.

The home computing lessons that Jasmine had provided for the people who had responded to flyers had gone well, and she had found the experience very interesting. To her surprise, one of the women had asked if she would consider teaching two of her friends as well, and had said that she would be willing to host such a venture at her house.

Jasmine agreed to provide an initial session so that they could try out the idea. They left it that afterwards the group could decide whether or not they wanted to carry on.

A couple more phone calls came in from people who wanted to book a session. Because Jasmine had only distributed flyers to streets that were within fifteen minutes' walk away, times for these appointments were relatively easy to fix up. She began to make notes for developing a series of simple handouts to augment her teaching. Personalised information was best, of course, but a backup of general points that kept coming up was bound to come in handy.

A call had also come in for help from a woman who had bought a new computer and was having difficulty with setting it up. Apparently her son had promised that he would come and do it once it had been delivered, but in the end it had turned out that he couldn't come for several weeks. Jasmine was able to deal with this assignment quite promptly, and the customer was delighted, declaring that she would keep Jasmine's phone number handy, and would recommend her to other local people.

At this stage, Jasmine began to wonder if she should distribute more flyers, thus increasing her chances of expanding this area of her work. However, she wasn't yet sure how much of her time she wanted to spend on it, so decided against any further advertising for now. There was her part-time employment with Snaith and Drew in Redchurch, and the occasional sessions at their main office. Clearly there was a market for home computing sessions locally. But she had found the work for the plumber extremely satisfying, and she hoped that in time she might find similar or even more challenging assignments. Perhaps this kind of service should feature prominently on her website. The general layout of a website for her business was becoming clearer and clearer to her, but she wasn't any nearer to choosing a name and then obtaining a suitable domain. Obviously, the work she did as a waitress would not feature on the site, and she could reduce the hours if her own business flourished to the point that she no longer had enough time.

Jasmine hadn't seen Maider for a while. They had kept in touch by phone, but Jasmine was now feeling guilty that her idea of going to Spanish classes had been far away from her mind, and added to that, there was no way that she could go to Spain with Maider this summer. She needed every penny that she could save, and at this stage she couldn't risk taking any time off.

She raised all this with Maider in their next phone conversation.

'Don't you worry,' her friend assured her. 'I'd worked all that out for myself. And actually, because you were so supportive I've managed to take a few steps forward.'

'I'm really glad to hear that. I was worried that me being distracted by my own preoccupations might have been holding you back.'

'Not at all. I've been meaning to tell you that I've managed to be upfront with Stephan about my worries of how I'll be if I go and visit them all, and he was great. He said he often still finds himself crying when he refers to his dad and my mum. I've promised him that I'll look for a cheap flight for mid-September. I just wanted to check with you first, and now I know for sure that you can't come this year, I'll go ahead and book something.'

'Sounds good,' said Jasmine.

'Maybe you'll be free to come another time,' Maider told her warmly. 'Stephan and Clover are definitely going to try to start a family, and I'm sure that an extra auntie will be welcome. Oh, and there's something else…'

'What's that?'

'Stephan's going to e-mail me some photos of sunflower fields when they're at their best.'

'That's wonderful!' exclaimed Jasmine spontaneously. 'You must let me see them.'

'I won't forget,' Maider promised. 'Now, tell me what you've been up to.'

Jasmine told her friend of Dad's offer of financial backing, and of her success with the plumber's paperwork.

'That's great news,' said Maider, 'and I bet you're glad to see the back of that project.'

'Well, actually, I'm not,' Jasmine replied. 'I know for a fact that I'm going to miss it.' There was complete silence at the other end of the phone, and Jasmine thought that the line had gone dead. Expecting to get no answer, she asked, 'Hello, are you still there?'

'I'm still here, but I'm gaping.'

'Why?'

'I don't know *anyone* who likes that sort of work.'

'Well, you do now.'

'Yes, you. Would you like me to pass your name on to someone I know?'

'Yes, of course. Who is it?'

'It's someone I made friends with when I was living with Tim. Her name's Sandra. Her husband's a farmer, and she's expected to do all the paperwork, but she hates it, and in any case, even without that she's pretty overloaded.'

'I could send you a photocopy of the testimonial I got from the plumber's wife,' Jasmine offered.

'Good. I'll give her a ring soon.'

'I'd really appreciate that.' Jasmine paused for a minute. There was something important in her mind, but she couldn't quite put her finger on it. Ah, now she had it! 'Maider, I've been trying to think of a logo for my business.'

'What are your ideas so far?'

'That's just it. I hadn't got any until…'

'Until when?'

'Until just after you were talking about photos of sunflower fields. Sunflowers are such a beautiful vibrant colour. I'd like to use them, or one, for my logo.'

'Well, you're so good at brightening up people's lives, I'm not surprised that you want to use sunflower imagery.'

'When I draw up the home page of my website, I'll experiment with some. Do you think Stephan would mind if I took material from his photos?'

'I'll ask him, but don't you want something soon?'

'Not necessarily. I'm only feeling my way at the moment, so although I'm gathering together ideas for my business name and domain name, I won't finalise them for a while yet.'

To her great surprise, Jasmine received a phone message from Maider's friend, Sandra, the following week.

The message said: 'Hi, I'm Sandra Green. Maider gave me your number. Can you ring me back?' And she had left a landline number. The voice sounded warm, cheerful and energetic.

Jasmine rang her as soon as she could, but the only reply was from a callminder. She left a brief message to say that she was returning Sandra's call and was looking forward to speaking to her.

She heard nothing more for a couple of days. Then her mobile rang on her way to picking up her lift at Snaith and Drew.

'Hello, Jasmine Simmons speaking.' These days she always tried to sound friendly but slightly formal, in case it was a business call.

'This is Sandra. I'm so glad I've caught you. A number of things intervened after I left my message, and delayed getting back to you. I understand that you're qualified in business studies and office management.'

'That's correct.'

'And that you've got some experience in reorganising a business in distress.'

'Well, I recently sorted out a long backlog of paperwork

for one,' said Jasmine truthfully.

'When would you be free to meet?' asked Sandra.

'I'm on my way to a job, but I'll get my diary out.'

Jasmine managed to clamp her mobile phone under the side of her chin as she located her diary and opened it.

'As soon as possible,' Sandra added.

Jasmine thought that she sounded rather agitated. 'Whereabouts are you?' she asked.

'We're out in the middle of nowhere,' replied Sandra. 'No, that's not quite true, but it feels like it at the moment. I'll start again. We're in the countryside about five miles from a village called Redchurch. Do you know it?'

'As a matter of fact, I'm working in Redchurch this morning,' Jasmine told her. 'I'll be at the new office of Snaith and Drew.'

'That's perfect!' exclaimed Sandra. 'We use Snaith and Drew. When can I pick you up?'

For Jasmine, this was going a bit too quickly. She was now standing at the bus stop, and could see her bus approaching. She thought quickly. 'I'm really sorry, but I'll have to ring off now,' she said. 'Can I call you in about fifteen minutes?'

'That would be perfect. Sorry if I was a bit pushy. I'll hear from you soon.'

The short bus ride to meet Mrs Reid, who was going to the Redchurch office that morning, allowed Jasmine to collect her thoughts. On the surface of it, the contact with Sandra sounded almost too good to be true. Her impulse was to say that she could be collected just after one that afternoon, but there was a niggle in her mind that she couldn't quite identify. Caution prevailed, and she decided to say that she had some time available later that afternoon, and could be collected around four if that suited. This would give her more time to prepare herself. At this stage she didn't know how she would get back home afterwards, but her free time in the afternoon would allow her to look into this. If necessary she could get a taxi to take her to a suitable bus route.

As soon as she stepped off the bus, she rang Sandra.

'Hello Sandra. I could be available around four at Redchurch,' she began.

'Any earlier?'

Jasmine thought that she now detected a hint of desperation in Sandra's voice, and she was tempted to respond to this by agreeing to an earlier time. But as thus far she knew nothing about the business proposition, she decided that it was better not to waver. 'I have some things to see to before that,' she replied, 'but I can be sure of being clear of them by four.'

'I'll be waiting outside the old post office for you. Look forward to meeting you.'

Jasmine switched off her phone and walked briskly to the office car park. Mrs Reid had just arrived, and waved across to her. Jasmine got into the front passenger seat and they set off for Redchurch.

They exchanged pleasantries on the journey. Jasmine always enjoyed this. When she had first taken up this post, she had imagined that the journeys with each of the partners would involve discussions about work, but they rarely did. Before they reached Redchurch that morning, Jasmine mentioned that she would not be travelling back to town that day. She wondered about explaining why.

While she was deliberating about this, Mrs Reid said pleasantly, 'I hope you've got something nice on.'

'Well, actually, it might be a chance of another work assignment,' Jasmine confided.

'That's good to hear.'

Jasmine decided to take the plunge and mention that it was a Snaith and Drew client who had contacted her. 'We have a mutual friend,' she added hastily, suddenly concerned that Mrs Reid might think that she had been using office information inappropriately. Out of the corner of her eye she could see that Mrs Reid was smiling.

'So you won't need a reference from us on this occasion,' she remarked.

'I suppose not,' Jasmine replied politely, 'but I'll remember to mention the possibility to Mrs Green.'

By now Mrs Reid was parking her car outside the old post office, and she said no more about the matter. After this, Jasmine managed to put out of her mind her impending contact with Sandra Green. She was pleased that she had made the decision to give herself a few hours between the end of the morning and that meeting. It meant that she could focus entirely on her work for Snaith and Drew.

The morning seemed to rush by, and just after one, Jasmine left the office with Mrs Reid, who locked the door behind them.

'I hope your meeting goes well,' Mrs Reid said to her before she drove away.

'Thank you,' Jasmine replied. She appreciated the interest that Mrs Reid had shown. It helped her to feel more confident.

The day was clear, with no sign of rain. There was a growing warmth in the sun, and Jasmine decided to walk along one of the roads out of the village while she ate the sandwich that she had brought in her bag. She wondered what kind of farm the Greens had. She wished now that she had asked Maider more about it. Too late for that now. She'd find out once she got there. Sandra certainly wanted help with paperwork, but from what she sensed from the phone call, the job might involve more than that.

She checked the time on her watch. It was a quarter to two. This meant that she still had a couple of hours free. It was quite unfamiliar being out on a country lane without anything that she *had* to do. For a moment she regretted her decision to stick to the four o'clock meeting time. Then she realised that this break was exactly what she needed, and that it was the kind of thing that had been missing from her life for the past months. She decided to spend another hour or so wandering along the road and back to Redchurch, and the rest of the time she could sit in the small café that was at the other end of the street from the old post office.

Back in Redchurch, Jasmine bought a magazine at the supermarket and also studied the bus timetable that was helpfully displayed on a notice board. Then she found a corner table in the café, where, while looking through the magazine, she enjoyed a hot drink. At ten to four, she left and walked briskly up the street, where she found a Land Rover waiting outside the office. She went round to the driver's window.

'Are you Sandra Green?' she asked the woman in the driver's seat, who she guessed must be about ten years older than herself.

'Yes, I am. And you must be Jasmine Simmons. Jump in.'

Jasmine climbed into the passenger seat, and Sandra drove off. Jasmine noticed that she accelerated much faster than anyone else she knew.

'I think I'd better cut the preliminaries and get straight to the point,' Sandra announced.

'That's fine with me,' Jasmine replied.

Sandra did not hesitate. 'It's the end of the financial year. Our office is a room in the farmhouse. It's a total mess. We've been letting the paperwork slide, and over the past year it's got worse than ever before. We've got three youngish children, and the middle one has developed a medical problem that's going to take up a lot of my time over the next months. We desperately need someone who'll put everything in the office to rights, and put things into shape for the future.'

'Maybe we could start by you showing me the room,' Jasmine suggested.

'Okay, but prepare for a shock,' Sandra warned. She

jammed on the brakes, and turned sharp left into what Jasmine could see was the drive up to the farmhouse. She glimpsed a sign at the corner. Restharrow Farm.

As Sandra parked, Jasmine could see through a front window that three children were clustered in front of a large television screen.

'Dan's not far away,' Sandra commented, as if aware of Jasmine's inner reaction to observing the children.

Sandra led the way through a side door into the building, and stopped at a closed door at the end of a short passageway. 'Prepare yourself,' she repeated, without emotion.

She opened the door, and Jasmine had to stifle a gasp. The floor of the small room was nearly completely invisible. The desk that was placed against one wall was piled high with files, and underneath it were jammed a number of supermarket shopping bags, stuffed to the brim with documents. The opposite wall was shelved from floor to ceiling, and every one of the shelves was packed with a mixture of loose letters, untidy files, and what appeared to be a number of instruction manuals.

'Mum!' a child's voice wailed from nearby.

'I'll have to go,' said Sandra. 'Can you have a look? I'll be back in about half an hour.'

'That's all right,' replied Jasmine.

Alone, as she surveyed the confusion, she felt daunted. How on earth could anyone do anything with this mess? And if they did manage, it would have taken forever. Well, here she was, and she'd better get on with assessing the real size of the problem.

She moved a tottering pile of packets from the one ancient wooden chair, and perched gingerly on the edge of it. It creaked, and rocked a little. Closer examination revealed that the legs were working loose. She made a mental note to keep an eye on this. She wished that she had an overall with her.

Then she noticed that there was a bag hanging from a hook at the back of the door, and inside it she found some old rags. Thank goodness they seemed to be clean enough! After that she set to work cleaning dirt off files from the floor, and stacking them in even piles at the back of the desk. Some had dried hen droppings on them. She spotted a rusty old knife on the narrow window ledge, and used it to scrape the mess off into an empty plastic container that looked as if it could be used as a litter bin.

There was no sign of Sandra's return, and Jasmine lost track of time. By the time she looked at her watch it was six thirty. It was then that Sandra came back. She was carrying a child, who was burying his face in her shoulder.

'Look,' she said. 'I'm really sorry, but everything's gone pear-shaped. Could you possibly stay until Dan's finished? He could run you home after that, and you can talk to him in the car.'

Under such fraught circumstances, Jasmine didn't feel she had any option but to agree. In addition she imagined that Sandra would have no idea at all when Dan would be coming in, and she was tempted not to ask. However, she resisted this.

'What time is that likely to be?' she asked as casually as she could.

'Around eight, if I'm to be honest,' Sandra told her apologetically.

'Okay. I'll text home to say I'll be late in.'

Sandra disappeared, and Jasmine sent a text to Mum before settling back into the gargantuan task that faced her.

After a while she thought that she heard light footsteps in the corridor, and she opened the door to find a boy who was carrying a large plastic bottle of lemonade, a chunky earthenware mug and a small plastic carrier bag with something in it.

'Mum told me to bring these,' he announced.

'Thanks very much,' said Jasmine as she took them and

put them on the desk. 'I'm Jasmine. What's your name?'

'Robert.'

'And how old are you?'

'Nearly ten. My brother's eight and my sister's six. My brother's ill.'

'I'm sorry to hear about that.'

Robert gave no sign of going away.

'Would you like to stay for a while?' asked Jasmine.

Robert nodded.

'I've only got one chair. Can you bring a stool from somewhere? And if you bring another mug, we can share the lemonade.'

Robert turned and disappeared. While he was away, Jasmine looked in the plastic bag and found two rolls with egg filling. Robert was back soon, carrying a battered-looking four-legged stool, and had a plastic mug hooked on to one of his fingers. He sat down and surveyed the scene.

'It looks a lot better already,' he commented.

'Thanks, but there's a long way still to go.'

Robert digested this piece of information.

'I'm doing the cleaning first,' Jasmine explained, 'but at the same time I'm having a look to see what it is that I'm cleaning, and how old it is. That means I can arrange things in different heaps, ready to work on later.'

'Can I help?' he asked.

'Yes, of course.' Jasmine pointed to the bag behind the door. 'Choose a rag out of there.'

Robert stood on the stool to select one. 'This is a piece of Dad's old pyjamas,' he pronounced triumphantly. 'Now, where shall I start?'

'Let's have a drink first, and we can share these egg rolls,' Jasmine suggested.

After this, they worked side-by-side with the cleaning, and she showed Robert how to look for dates in the files and clues as to what the documents were about.

The time passed companionably, and when someone

else came to the door, it took Jasmine by surprise.

'It's Dad!' shouted Robert. He dropped the file he was working on and jumped straight into his father's arms.

'I didn't know you had become an office assistant,' said Dan playfully. He turned to Jasmine. 'Hi, I'm Dan.'

'Glad to meet you,' said Jasmine politely. Her hands were full of files.

'You can't possibly be as glad as I am to meet *you*,' Dan replied sincerely. 'Look, I'm sorry. It's terribly late.'

'What time is it?' asked Jasmine.

'It's long after eight. We'd better get going.'

'Can I come?' asked Robert.

'I'm afraid not,' Dan replied. 'You've got a school day tomorrow.'

'Bah!' Robert exclaimed crossly, and ran off along the corridor.

'Grab your things and jump into the Land Rover. I'll say goodnight to the kids and be with you in a minute.'

Soon Dan was in the Land Rover beside her, and Jasmine noticed that his style of acceleration was almost identical to Sandra's.

'What are your terms?' Dan asked bluntly.

Jasmine froze. Her head was full of the systems that she intended to implement.

'What do you charge?' Dan asked, a little louder.

'Er...'

'I'm sorry. I'm making it sound too simple. It's not, is it?'

'No. Not at all.' Having said this, Jasmine felt back on track. 'You see, it depends on what you want. I could organise everything, put systems in place, and then you can take over from there, or I could go on to prepare all the material for your accountant.'

'It's the full works we're after.'

'There's the issue of my availability, and we've got to take into account that I don't have my own transport.'

'Name your price,' said Dan. There was a terse edge to his voice, born of desperation.

Jasmine longed to make the lives of this family easier. She was about to say she was sure that they could sort something out, when something stopped her. Dad had promised to help her financially if she hadn't got sufficient income. However, she didn't want to rely on that and end up undercharging Sandra and Dan. Added to this she longed to feel confident about moving into a financially independent position. Handling the negotiations appropriately with Dan was an important step.

'I think that the best thing would be if I work out an estimate for the first phase of the work,' she told him.

'But won't that delay a start date?' he pressed.

'Not necessarily. I can offer an hourly rate at first. At the moment I'm working in Redchurch two mornings a week – Tuesdays and Thursdays. On those days, I could take a lunch break and then work in your office after that, if someone can collect me from Redchurch.'

Dan thought about this. 'And if you can stay late, I can take you straight home afterwards. Otherwise, someone can run you back to Redchurch to catch the bus.'

'In general I'll probably be able to stay on, but there will be times when I'll have to leave in time to catch the six o'clock bus from Redchurch.'

Dan acknowledged this with a grunt, and then added, 'Can I take it that you're willing to come back early next week?'

'I think I should be able to, but I'll have to check. I can give Sandra a ring tomorrow. I've got her number.'

'I'll give you mine when I drop you off.' Dan was quiet for a moment, and then said, as if to himself, 'I'll need to get a laptop in there for you.'

After this he spent some time explaining how things had got in such a mess. The combination of ageing relatives needing help, taking on extra projects on the farm, and now his son's illness, had put a burden on him of unforeseen proportions. It was clear that he felt deeply unhappy about the chaos in the office room, the door of which he had kept shut in a futile attempt to ignore the inevitable.

Lying in bed that night, Jasmine reflected on this rather unexpected turn of events. She had never imagined that the job for the Greens would have presented quite like this. It might provide her with work for some time to come. What hours could she offer them? Realistically, the simplest thing would definitely be to work there for the afternoon and part of the evening twice a week, as this fitted in so well with her work in Redchurch.

But supposing they wanted her to pull round the mess more quickly than that arrangement would allow? How could she fit in more time? Jasmine began to feel quite stressed as she thought of this. For one thing, the travelling would be more awkward, and for another, she wasn't sure that she would be left with enough time to see to everything else.

Then she remembered how stressed Sandra was, and the note of desperation that had crept into Dan's voice when he was bringing her home that evening. She just *had* to help them as much as she possibly could. Jasmine broke out in a sweat.

It was soon after this that she realised two things. The first was entirely practical. If necessary she could ask Dan to transport some boxfuls of the paperwork each time he brought her home, and that would mean she could advance things in any spare time she had available.

The second was a completely different aspect of the whole picture. The Greens had two boys and a girl, and she had two brothers and a sister. She knew that she had always kept an eye on her siblings, not exactly like a parent, but like a parent-helper – someone who tried to fill in some of the gaps. And it was only recently that she had realised that she could now let go of that role. Could it be that some of her panic about the Green's situation wasn't to do with them at all? After all, she had only just met them, so why should she feel so worried about their situation? And why should she feel that it was *up to her* to make it all right for them?

After forming these questions, she relaxed, and soon fell sleep.

Chapter Fourteen

The next morning, Jasmine woke feeling completely calm. It was Friday, and she had a long shift at the restaurant that evening, starting at six thirty. She wanted to fit in a swim today at the local pool. Because swimming always left her feeling refreshed, she made a mental note to try to go a bit more often.

Her mind was clear about what to say to Dan Green, and she decided to ring him straight after breakfast.

She ate a piece of toast, packed her swimming things, and rang Dan's number. There was no reply, so she left a brief but detailed message.

'Hi, this is Jasmine Simmons phoning to confirm that I'll do two until about eight on Tuesdays and Thursdays. I suggest we stick to my hourly rate until I'm in a better position to see the whole picture. If that's okay with you, I'll be outside the old post office in Redchurch at one thirty next Tuesday.'

After this, she decided to take the rest of the morning off. This would allow enough time to walk to the pool and back as well as having a good swim. It wasn't exactly time off, though. She knew that spending the morning doing something very physical would give her a context in which she could organise more of her thoughts about various developments in her work schedule.

The pool was about two miles away, and if she took the route along where the railway used to be, the walk was very pleasant. She popped a notebook and pencil into the bag with her swimming things, and set off. As she walked along, she found herself humming a cheerful tune. She couldn't remember where she had heard it, but that didn't matter.

She enjoyed her swim. The pool was quite quiet that morning. Although normally the bustle of the many users of the pool was something that Jasmine rather liked, today she valued being able to concentrate largely on her inner thoughts. Somehow the rhythm of her strokes enabled her mind to contemplate things one at a time.

Returning home by the same route, Jasmine was aware that although she hadn't made any particular decisions, somehow everything in her life seemed more ordered, and she felt energised. Nearing the house, she checked her mobile and found a text from Dan Green, which said: Fine, Dan.

The message couldn't have been more brief, but it was entirely to the point. She imagined that he had sent it while rushing from one job to another. She wondered how his middle child was now. No doubt she would learn something on Tuesday. So far she only knew the name of Robert, the oldest child, but Tuesday would also provide an opportunity for her to ask for the other names. Then she pulled herself up. Yes, these things were a part of the life that would surround her at the farm, but her role there was not really to familiarise herself with the family and its dynamics.

Jasmine was full of eager anticipation when she jumped out of bed on Tuesday morning. She was looking forward to the morning's work in Redchurch, and then the challenge at Restharrow Farm.

After leaving work, she had some lunch at the little café. The vegetable soup was excellent, and the warm brown rolls were very filling. She was back outside the old post office several minutes in advance of the agreed collection time, and soon saw the now familiar Land Rover coming into view. The vehicle was certainly familiar, but it turned out that the driver was not. As he stopped alongside her, he ran the window down.

'Are you Ms Simmons?' he asked.

'Yes, I'm waiting for Dan or Sandra Green.'

'I'm Jim. Dan asked me to come for you.'

Jasmine hesitated. No one had let her know about this.

Jim seemed to understand her dilemma and added, 'Ring Dan's mobile if you want.'

Jasmine made her decision. 'I don't think that'll be necessary.' She climbed into the passenger seat. 'Do you work at Restharrow Farm?' she asked.

'Sometimes. I'm a relief tractor man. I'm shared between several farms.'

Nothing further was said until Jim dropped her off at the farmhouse.

'The door's not locked,' he called as he turned the Land Rover. Then he sped away up the drive and out of sight.

Inside the house everything was completely silent. Jasmine was certain that there was no one there. It wasn't yet two o'clock, but she went straight to the office room.

When she opened the door, she had an enormous surprise. The difference from how it had been when she had left it on Thursday evening was remarkable. The floor was clean and was completely clear of everything, and there was an addition to the furniture. As well as the desk, its chair and the stool, there was an old-fashioned cupboard that had been placed under the window.

The desk had on it only a small laptop and one stack of files. Although some of the files were stained, they were all clean. Everything on the shelves on the opposite wall looked neat and clean.

She went over to the cupboard and opened its doors. Ah! This was where everything from the floor had been put, together with nearly all the files that she'd left stacked on the desk. All of this looked neat and clean.

Jasmine opened the laptop and switched it on. She guessed that it must be about a couple of years old. It was easy for her find her way round it. Now she could make a start on the lengthy task of cataloguing everything. She decided to work through the contents of the cupboard first, and soon found that there was some kind of logic in the way in which things were arranged. Although the system was not without flaws, the simple sense of it surprised her. Its main feature was a fairly consistent attempt at following a date order, and some attention had been paid to subject matter. There was also a motley selection of documents that appeared to have nothing at all to do with the farm.

How strange. Jasmine was certain that neither Dan nor Sandra could have had time to make all these changes, so who had? There was no answer to that question, at least for now, and she focused on her cataloguing task.

More than two hours passed, and then suddenly the door opened and Robert was standing there with a wide grin on his face.

'Hi!' he greeted her.

'Hello again,' Jasmine replied. 'Have you just come back from school?'

Robert did not answer. Instead he asked, 'What do you think?'

'What do I think about what?'

'The room, of course.'

'I wondered who had been in here. Was it you?'

Robert nodded proudly. 'I've been in here for *ages and ages* since you went away.'

'You did *all this*!' exclaimed Jasmine incredulously.

Robert beamed at her. 'It was nearly all me. My sister, Amy, cleaned the floor, but I did all the rest.'

'Goodness! Did you live in here after I went away?' Jasmine joked.

'Yes,' replied Robert seriously. 'I swept a bit of the floor and put my sleeping bag there. As soon as I woke up the next morning, I did some work before I went to school, and when I came back I started again. Mum and Dad didn't try to stop me. I think they were glad I was doing something useful.'

'You've done really well.'

'I can't help today, though. Mum's at the hospital with my brother, Ian, and one of her friends has brought us home with her children until she gets back. I'm off to play with them.'

He disappeared down the corridor, and Jasmine settled back into her work. Apart from distant sounds of peels of laughter and an occasional thud or two, everything was peaceful, and again absorbed in her task, Jasmine lost track of time.

Much later, Robert reappeared. This time he was carrying food and drink.

'Mum's back now,' he informed her, 'so the others have gone. Here, this is for you. I'd like to help again soon. You can teach me some more things.'

Jasmine's work at Restharrow Farm quickly fell into a pleasant routine. Only rarely did she have to change her Tuesday and Thursday times, and there were occasional weeks when she was persuaded to fit in a whole Wednesday as well. On these occasions the children insisted that she had to stay overnight on the Tuesday and Wednesday, too. This she was happy to do. Not only did it cut down the travelling time, but also they had a lot of fun. There were even a couple of times when the children sent Dan and Sandra out to see some of their friends, and made Jasmine read to them before they went to bed.

Chapter Fifteen

At home, there was a considerable amount of grumbling coming from Norrie and Blake, and it tended to be directed towards Jasmine. At times they behaved like small children, complaining bitterly about Restharrow Farm having stolen her. Then they would move on to recounting tales of invasions by people viewing their home. After that they would retreat to their room, making sure that they 'accidentally' banged against the wall that separated their room from hers. If she went in and asked what the problem was, they would deny everything and say that they were 'just working'.

By contrast, Poppy's behaviour seemed exemplary. In Jasmine's frequent absences she helped Mum a lot in the kitchen, and she was much firmer than usual with Tippy. In fact, all in all, she appeared to be more grown-up.

School finished for the summer, and Mum put pressure on the boys to sort through everything in their room, insisting that she was not willing to take any rubbish when they moved house. Jasmine learned from Mum that it was now certain they would be moving to the police house. However, it was still not clear exactly when they would be going. There had been an increasing amount of interest in their home, but as yet, no one had placed a firm offer. Mum and Dad were showing signs of stress about this, but there was nothing that could be done to hurry things along.

Jasmine's income was now adequate to fund living elsewhere. There was the money from Snaith and Drew, and from the restaurant. In addition, Dan and Sandra had offered her a contract for six months. At first she had questioned this, saying she wasn't sure that she would be needed for so long. Dan and Sandra had assured her that they had no doubt about it, and that if funds allowed, they hoped to offer her work beyond that, too. In between all of this she fitted in the home computing lessons. With her financial position more stable, Jasmine concentrated more time on finding suitable accommodation.

It was when she was doing a day's cover at Snaith and Drew's main office that Jasmine heard of something interesting. It was Megan who told her about it.

'You know you told me that your family will be moving away later this year,' she began.

'Yes,' Jasmine replied.

'Well, I thought I'd let you know about the flat above here.'

Jasmine knew that the floor immediately above the office was used by the owner of the whole building, and that he was called Ewan Gallagher. It seemed that he was hardly ever there, though.

'You don't mean Mr Gallagher's residence?' she asked.

'No, I mean the floor above – the attic.'

Surprised, Jasmine said, 'I didn't know there was anyone there.'

'There isn't. Well, not yet anyway. Jasmine, I've heard that Ewan is going to let it out. He's only in his flat for a couple of days here and there, but he does like his peace. I gather he's going to try letting out the attic flat, so long as he can find quiet people.'

'Is it an actual flat?' asked Jasmine curiously.

'Yes, I believe it was created at the same time as the whole building was changed from a family home, but as far as I'm aware, it's never been occupied.'

'How can I find out more about it?'

'We've been asked to advertise and be the point of contact for potential tenants, although someone else will be doing the viewing and interviewing.'

Megan took a sheet of paper out of a folder and handed it to Jasmine, who studied it eagerly.

'Three bedrooms,' she murmured. That would mean she would have two companions. She read on. 'Bathroom, kitchen, living room, separate toilet.' The price was surprisingly reasonable.

As if reading her mind, Megan said, 'I understand that he won't tolerate anyone who isn't prepared to live like he does – no noise, no alcohol and that kind of thing.'

'Suits me,' Jasmine stated. 'You've got my contact details already. Please put me right at the top of your list.'

Megan smiled. 'I hope you're selected. It'll be really nice to know that you're living above here.'

Only two weeks later, Jasmine received a call on her mobile from the agent who was in charge of the let, and she made an appointment to see the flat and discuss the terms and conditions.

The day of the appointment came. While she was waiting for the agent to arrive, Jasmine did something that she had never thought of doing before. She walked round the outside of the building several times, counting the windows on the first floor and the attic floor, and noting the size and position of them. Then she stood as far back as possible to see what view of the roof and guttering she could get. However nice the situation of the flat was, the last thing she wanted to have to worry about was the idea of water dripping into her bedroom! As she had expected, everything appeared to be in very good order, but she made a mental note to find out how repairs should be reported and carried out.

The agent arrived exactly on time, and introduced himself as Mr Wood. Although she guessed that he was in his forties, his formal way of conducting himself was that of an older person. He took her round the back of the building and let her in by the rear door. Jasmine had been through this door before as there was access to a small room in which the office cleaning materials were stored. She had known that there was another door there, but had never given any thought to where it led. Mr Wood unlocked it to reveal a carpeted staircase.

'This is a shared access to Mr Gallagher's flat and the one above,' he explained.

'I knew about the internal one from Snaith and Drew's office,' Jasmine told him, adding quickly, 'I've worked there for a while. I've seen Mr Gallagher coming through occasionally, but I've never officially met him.'

Mr Wood said nothing, and led the way to the first floor.

The attic flat was accessed by a narrow stairway that went up from a tiny landing at the rear of Mr Gallagher's flat. No wonder he wanted to be certain about the kind of neighbours he was going to have, thought Jasmine, as the agent took her up. Not only would they be directly above him, but also they would pass close to the back of his flat. And with that shared back staircase there was also an issue of security.

At the top of the stairs was a lightwell with a wide walkway round it. Mr Wood used another key to open the door to the flat, and invited Jasmine to go in.

Jasmine fell in love with it straight away. Its square rooms with old-fashioned well-worn furniture looked inviting, and there was one bedroom in particular that she liked.

Mr Wood gave her a little time to wander round while he laid out on the kitchen table the contents of a file that he had brought with him. Then he went to get her.

He cleared his throat. 'Please take a seat,' he began. 'Mr Gallagher is looking for a particular kind of tenant.'

'Yes, Mrs Cowan mentioned this.'

Silently, Mr Wood handed a sheet across to her. It was headed 'Essential Criteria'.

Jasmine read through everything, and then smiled at Mr

Wood. 'I would have no difficulty in doing my part to ensure that Mr Gallagher is not disturbed.'

Mr Wood seemed to relax slightly. 'The rest of the terms and conditions are fairly standard. We need two references and the deposit as stated.'

Jasmine had noted the figure. It was higher than she had expected, but despite the fact that Dad had offered to pay it all, she knew that she would be able to fund at least half of it.

'One of my references will be from Snaith and Drew,' she said confidently, 'and I'll arrange another shortly.' She was certain that Sandra and Dan would provide one. How fortunate it was that as well as working from there she had stayed with them at times.

'I have several other people who are interested in the flat,' Mr Wood said rather stiffly. Then he added, 'But I'll certainly put your name forward to Mr Gallagher.'

'I'll get my references to you promptly,' Jasmine assured him. 'How soon after that will I know if I've got a place?'

'I'm afraid I'm not able to tell you that, but I do know that Mr Gallagher is aiming to have the flat occupied by early to mid-August.'

As far as Jasmine was concerned that couldn't be more perfect.

Mr Wood consulted his watch rather pointedly. 'I'll show you out,' he said firmly.

They went down the stairs in silence, and after they had left the building, he locked the door. He shook hands with her, but Jasmine felt no sense of this being a communication. He smiled equally mechanically, and then strode off towards the front of the building. Jasmine headed straight down the drive and out on to the street.

When she arrived home, Poppy and Mum were in the kitchen, having a mug of tea and a chat. Jasmine joined them eagerly, keen to tell them how things had gone.

'Will I be able to come and stay?' asked Poppy. She

was clearly excited.

'I don't see why not,' Jasmine replied. 'I saw a fold-up bed in a large storage cupboard, and all the bedrooms are big enough. Of course, everything depends on whether or not I get a place.'

'Mr Gallagher couldn't have a better neighbour,' Mum remarked.

Poppy persisted. 'If you don't get a place in that flat, can I come and stay wherever you are?'

'I'd like that very much,' said Jasmine warmly.

Poppy looked pleased. Tippy was trying to jump up on to her knee, and she fended him off.

Chapter Sixteen

Things were falling into place. Jasmine had secured a room in Ewan Gallagher's attic flat, and was going to move in during the first week of August. And at last Mum and Dad had a buyer for their house. The only snag was that the new owners could not take it over until October.

It was soon decided that Norrie and Blake would move in with Dad at the police house for the start of the school term. It was obvious that this was the most sensible course of action, as it was imperative that their studies were not disrupted. The only remaining problem was Poppy's situation. She was adamant that she didn't want to move until Mum came too, and that meant she would have to start the term at her existing school, and then move after a few weeks. Dad contacted the schools about this, and he found that because she was only at second year level, it could be accommodated. Tippy would stay with Poppy and Mum until the final move was made.

Jasmine was surprised about how happy she felt with these arrangements. She realised it meant a lot to her that Mum, Poppy and Tippy would be nearby for a bit longer than she had expected. However, she said nothing about this. She was very excited about the prospect of meeting her new flatmates in only a few weeks' time.

As August came closer, Jasmine arranged with Dad that he would help her to move her things during the first weekend. She was surprised when Norrie and Blake insisted on being involved, too. Poppy and Mum collected together a number of strong cardboard boxes for Jasmine to pack her things in.

When the great day came, the whole family did all

they could to help. Poppy produced a small pot plant that she had bought with her pocket money, and presented it to Jasmine for her new room.

The flat was quite busy because other boxes were being delivered. Apparently their owner was due to arrive the following day. Overall, everything went smoothly, and by evening, Jasmine's room was already looking comfortable and welcoming. She had opted to cook her first meal alone, so the others left her to sample her new life. Of course, Mum and Poppy promised to phone her later on.

To Jasmine, it was very strange indeed being the only person in a large building. Yet it was not unpleasant. In fact, she became aware of a sense of warm anticipation of what the future might hold. And from now on, Tuesday and Thursday mornings would see her going downstairs and straight into the car of whoever was going to Redchurch that day.

Eager to get on with something, her mind filled with a sudden urge to work on materials for her business. The task of finalising a design for her business cards and her website was now long overdue. Maider had found out from Stephan that he was more than happy for Jasmine to use any of his sunflower photographs, and she spent the evening looking through them on her computer, identifying exactly what to use.

The next resident arrived around lunchtime the following day. Out of the living-room window Jasmine noticed a car draw up in front of the building. After a few minutes, a young woman appeared out of the passenger side, and waved goodbye to the driver before heading round the back, out of Jasmine's sight.

Soon Jasmine heard footsteps outside the door of the flat. She had an impulse to rush and open the door, but decided that she should wait and let the new person make her own way in. She went to the kitchen and put the kettle on.

When her flatmate came into the room she turned and smiled. 'Hi, I'm Jasmine,' she greeted her.

'I'm Bryony. It's good to meet you, and to be honest it's quite nice to find that there's someone here already. I thought I'd be on my own until the start of the week, and I wasn't looking forward to that.'

'I arrived yesterday, but my family is still living fairly close by. They helped me to move in.'

'Have you any idea who else is coming?' asked Bryony.

'I've heard it's another woman, but that's all,' Jasmine replied. 'Have you come far?'

'Not really. Just from another flat in town. The owner is moving back into it, so we all had to find somewhere else.'

'How many were there?'

'There were four of us. Actually, it was the right time for a change. The others were starting to settle down with regular partners, and I was feeling the odd one out. I think I'll keep in touch with two of them, though.'

'I was living at home, but my family are moving quite soon.'

'What's your work?'

'It's quite mixed – part-time office work, waitress, and I'm self-employed, too.'

'Interesting. I'm a trainee accountant, but I've got ambitions.'

'Accountancy sounds good. Part of my work includes some. Maybe I could pick your brains occasionally.'

'Pick away as often as you like,' Bryony invited. 'It's good practice for me to do a bit of teaching.'

'I wouldn't want to lean on you,' said Jasmine cautiously. 'We should find a way of doing swops. How are you with advanced IT skills?'

'That's just it,' Bryony replied. 'I'm pretty crap at that, and it's holding me back.'

'Oh good. Oh... I didn't mean...' Jasmine's voice trailed off.

'It's okay. I'm not taking offence,' Bryony assured her. 'Are you trying to say that you can help me?'

Jasmine nodded. 'It sounds as if we could be heading for a useful swop.'

The conversation then went on to more general subjects, and time flowed by until Bryony caught sight of the clock on the wall.

'Goodness!' she exclaimed. 'Where has the time gone? I'd better unpack.' She giggled and added, 'At the very least I'll need to find my night clothes and something to wear for work tomorrow.'

'I've got things I must get on with, too,' said Jasmine. 'Maybe I'll see you later on. Perhaps we can cook together?'

'Okay.'

'That's good.'

'After tonight, you won't see all that much of me,' Bryony informed her. 'I'm a bit of a workaholic, and I usually study in the evenings.'

'We can always book some time together when we want to do our first skills swop,' Jasmine suggested.

'That's a sensible plan,' Bryony agreed.

From her own room, Jasmine could hear a series of muffled thuds from Bryony's. She thought how this reminded her of being next to Norrie and Blake, although she imagined that Bryony's thuds wouldn't go on past today. Then once again she became absorbed in designing her business cards, and her awareness of everything else faded.

The shared meal was very pleasant. Making the food together was fun, and it tasted delicious. Jasmine and Bryony had some good laughs together, and when they parted, Jasmine felt even more relaxed than after a swim.

However, that night Jasmine felt unsettled. Her feelings were disturbed in an intangible kind of way, and the pain in her abdomen was back, albeit not so severely. Eventually she got off to sleep, but when morning came she was glad that she didn't have to get up straight away. She heard the door of the flat bang shut around eight thirty, and must have dozed off again because the next time she looked at her watch it was nearly ten.

Soon afterwards, she promised herself that she would finalise the design for her business cards and arrange to have some printed. The afternoon and early evening would be taken up with several home-computing lessons.

Chapter Seventeen

Jasmine soon got into the swing of conducting her working life from her room in the flat. She loved the feeling of being in an independent setting. This surprised her, because although she had felt ready to leave home, she had always imagined that it would be quite a wrench. She missed the others, but because of the way her life had been over the past months, she had seen less and less of them even though she had been sharing the same house.

Internet access was already in place when she had moved into the flat, and this meant that she could get on with things. In the end she had decided to continue using the name 'Office Support Services'. It was simple and professional. The sunflowers that she put on the home page of her website looked good.

She and Bryony learned that the arrival of the other occupant of the flat had been delayed by a few weeks. This was rather a surprise to them, but they concluded that it must be for a good reason.

When the end of August came, Jasmine went to share a final meal with the whole family, in the house that they had always lived in. Norrie and Blake had done quite a bit of research about their new school, and were feeling so enthusiastic about the opportunities it offered that they almost forgot to moan about the inconvenience of moving home. Poppy was showing signs of being pleased about having a few weeks with Mum all to herself. She continued to be firm with Tippy, who seemed to accept the change without protest.

The new flatmate arrived the day after Norrie and Blake

and Dad had set off to live in the police house together. Jasmine had had her lunch, and she was on her way out to give computing lessons for the afternoon, when she encountered a woman with a sizeable shoulder bag and a large flight bag on wheels. To Jasmine she looked a little older than herself and Bryony.

She held out her hand. 'Hello, I'm Jasmine. You must be our new flatmate. I'm on my way out to work. Sorry I can't stop, but I'll see you this evening.'

The new arrival took her hand. 'Yes, I'm the delayed flatmate. My name's Rosemary. I might not see you later today. I'm completely exhausted.'

'I'll catch up with you some time later, then,' said Jasmine as she hurried down the stairs.

As things turned out, it was the weekend before Jasmine was able to spend time with her flatmates. She was away from Tuesday morning to Thursday evening as she had stayed two nights at Sandra and Dan's, and Friday evening was spent working at the restaurant. By the time she saw Bryony and Rosemary at breakfast on Saturday morning, the two had got to know each other a little.

'Sorry I haven't been around,' Jasmine greeted them.

Rosemary smiled. 'If you had been, you would probably have been on your own.'

'Yes,' agreed Bryony, 'when I've not been at work, I've been up to the eyes in my studies. Apart from introducing myself outside the bathroom earlier this week, I didn't see Rosemary until yesterday evening.'

'We ended up eating together,' said Rosemary. 'It was good to have a bit of pleasant company after the turmoil of recent weeks.'

Rosemary said nothing about what the turmoil had been, and Jasmine did not ask.

Bryony turned to Rosemary. 'Actually, you did me a big favour.'

Rosemary looked puzzled. 'What was that?'

'I've been so tied up with my studies that sometimes I go to bed at night and then realise I haven't eaten anything.' She chuckled. 'But I definitely ate something yesterday evening.'

Jasmine felt concerned that Bryony had such a lighthearted attitude towards her failures to eat. She was on the thin side of slender, and in Jasmine's view shouldn't risk getting any thinner.

Aloud, she said, 'I expect that once we've all settled in properly we'll be able to get into some kind of routine.'

'Sounds about right,' Rosemary agreed. 'I'm not good with rigid patterns, but an informal routine that we can all work round would suit me.'

'Don't expect me to remember what it is,' Bryony warned playfully.

'It might help prompt your hunger buttons if some delicious aromas float out of the kitchen and waft under the door of your room,' Jasmine teased.

Bryony considered this with a serious expression on her face. 'Joking apart, I do probably need to be more on the ball about my eating habits. In the flat I came from, the others had taken to eating with their partners-to-be. Not only did this result in me being left out, but also it meant that my tendency to forget to eat really got a hold.'

'Time for a change for the better!' said Rosemary cheerfully.

'Fattening myself up will mean that I've got more clothes to choose from,' mused Bryony. 'I've shrunk out of a lot of my favourites.'

'No chance of that for me,' Rosemary stated. 'I love my food, and there's absolutely no way I'd forget a meal.'

'The way my work is at the moment, I'm often out until fairly late in the evening,' Jasmine explained. 'And Friday and Saturday I always eat something at the restaurant where I do waitressing.'

'Cordon bleu?' asked Rosemary.

'Not exactly,' Jasmine replied. 'We usually have pasta with something mixed in with it. It gives us energy for all the hours we spend on our feet.'

'Not even a human version of a posh doggy bag?'

Jasmine shook her head. 'It's against the rules.' She thought for a moment, and then said, 'Monday is the day when I'm most likely to be around to cook a proper evening meal.'

'I'd hate to have a fixed arrangement every evening,' Bryony reflected.

'We could pick one evening each to break up the week,' Rosemary suggested.

'And even then we can be flexible,' added Jasmine.

'Okay, it's a deal,' Bryony agreed. 'That way it means we get together sometimes and can exchange news and views.'

'And you won't lose any more weight,' Rosemary stated, wagging her finger with mock severity.

Bryony pulled a fake sour face, which resulted in the three of them collapsing with laughter.

When Rosemary could speak again, she said, 'I've got a wedding to go to in a couple of months' time, and my preferred dress is a bit on the tight side at the moment. Perhaps we could combine fattening Bryony with engineering a little shrinkage for me.'

The three of them found this to be hilarious.

While Jasmine and Bryony were still shaking with laughter, Rosemary went on. 'But one thing's for certain. Don't even *think* of suggesting that we follow some ridiculous eating plan out of a magazine.'

'There's no risk of that as far as I'm concerned,' Jasmine told her.

'I'm not a magazine fan,' Bryony announced. 'If I do flip through one, I certainly don't waste my time looking at instructions on how to decorate custard, and what size of bowl to eat from.'

Again this resulted in much laughter.

When Jasmine had recovered a little, she turned to Rosemary and said, 'By the way, there might be another way of going about the wedding dilemma.'

Rosemary looked interested. 'What's that?'

'I haven't done any sewing recently, but I don't think I'll have lost my skills. We could have a look at your dress together and see if there's enough in the seams to let it out a little,' Jasmine offered.

'Really?' said Rosemary. 'I'm hopeless at that sort of thing.'

'Why not go and get it and I can look at it for you now,' Jasmine suggested.

'It'll be coming with the rest of my stuff on Monday,' Rosemary told her. 'But I'd be really grateful if you'd have a look at it sometime. If you think you could adjust it, that would be great.'

'Put it in front of me next Saturday morning,' Jasmine advised. 'Don't forget.'

'Just how many skills have you got, Jasmine?' asked Bryony. 'Rosemary, she's already promised to help me with some advanced IT, and she seems to be juggling quite a range of jobs.'

'I'll be learning more about accountancy from you,' Jasmine reminded her. 'I like the fact that we've got different skills. It's going to come in handy.'

Bryony turned to Rosemary. 'What's your work?'

'I'm in the middle of changing career,' Rosemary explained. 'I was an assistant manager in a bank, but more and more I realised that I was in the wrong line of business. Then I decided I wanted to go into care work. I want to get a good range of practical hands-on experience first, and then eventually move into management. Of course I've had to take a big drop in income, but I know that this is the work that I really want to do.'

'I've got a friend from school who's a nurse,' said Jasmine. 'She's wondering about specialising in care of the elderly, but I'm not sure it would be entirely right for her. She's certainly really good with older people, and knows a lot about their needs.'

'How interesting,' replied Rosemary. 'Maybe I'll have a chance to meet her sometime.'

'I can invite her over once we're all properly settled in,' suggested Jasmine. 'The other person you might see here is my kid sister, Poppy. Before I moved in she was angling to come and stay for a night.'

Bryony smiled. 'I'd like that. My older sister has two girls. I sometimes go and stay for a long weekend, and I get on really well with my nieces. We have a lot of fun together, and I always miss them afterwards.'

'When I next speak to Poppy on the phone, I'll let her know that I've got an interested flatmate,' Jasmine promised.

Rosemary glanced at her watch. 'Oh!' she exclaimed, 'I've to be at the optometrist's for eleven to pick up my new glasses. I'll have to go.'

'Back to studying for me,' Bryony announced.

'I take it that I'll see you both on Monday evening, when I'll cook something for us all,' said Jasmine.

'That'll be great,' Rosemary replied appreciatively.

Bryony grinned. 'Good plan. And if I forget, you can waft something under my door, and I'll come rushing out.'

In the weeks that followed, Poppy came for tea on two Sundays. Rosemary didn't see her because she was committed to doing weekend cover for the placement she was on, but Bryony made a point of taking a break from her studies in order to spend some time with Poppy. They really hit it off together, and Jasmine enjoyed watching them interacting. In the past it had always been that she was a big sister, often in a mothering role, but while Bryony and Poppy were chatting, she could sit back and say very little. Poppy was certainly maturing, and Jasmine liked witnessing this.

Poppy didn't sleep over on either occasion. She claimed that Mum would miss her and that she couldn't leave her all on her own in the house. However, Jasmine knew that Mum was fine, and it was Poppy who was uncertain about being away from home overnight when the time of the final move was so near. In a way, she was relieved that Poppy didn't stay. More and more she realised that she needed to concentrate almost entirely on her new life.

As the day of the final move drew nearer and nearer, Jasmine spent a little time at her old home, helping Mum with some packing while Poppy was out saying a final goodbye to some of her school friends.

'These past weeks have been strange,' Mum told her, 'but I suppose this time has helped me to start getting used to the fact that the family has changed.'

'You mean that you've been getting used to me living somewhere else,' Jasmine corrected her.

'Yes, of course. I find it difficult to say straight out.' She stared at Jasmine with a stricken expression. 'I feel really happy for you, and I know it's the right thing, but it is a big wrench.'

Jasmine gave her a hug. 'I understand, but I feel it in a different kind of way.'

'I don't want my sadness to get in the way,' said Mum worriedly.

'It doesn't,' Jasmine assured her. 'I know that once you're set up in the police house, we'll both be looking forward to my first visit, and until then we'll be chatting on the phone as usual.'

The taut expression on Mum's face softened. 'You're right.'

After that, Mum showed Jasmine a few things from the kitchen that she thought she might like to have at her flat.

'Are you sure?' asked Jasmine. 'Won't you need them

yourself?'

'There's less cupboard space in the new kitchen, and in any case I'd like you to have them.'

'Well, thanks very much,' said Jasmine. 'I'll certainly make use of them. We try to cook a shared meal each every week, and I'm doing some experimenting.'

'That sounds a very good arrangement,' Mum approved.

Back at the flat that evening, Jasmine felt a bit strange, and found herself nibbling from a packet of biscuits that she had in her room. Later that week, the removal van would take everything from the family home, and Mum and Poppy would go by train. Tippy would be with them in his travelling cage.

Although she slept well, when she woke, Jasmine was aware of having had dreams of unfamiliar rooms – the same kind of rooms as before.

Chapter Eighteen

Everything was going fine. Jasmine's work had taken on a definite pattern. Putting more flyers through the letter boxes of people's homes and having her website live had resulted in more requests for computer home tuition, and also for troubleshooting. This meant that Mondays and Fridays were now largely filled. Tuesdays and Thursdays continued to be shared between the Redchurch branch of Snaith and Drew and the office at Restharrow Farm. The occasional addition of Wednesday was no longer necessary, but another farm in the locality had booked her services for every second Wednesday, and there was the chance of some employment at yet another farm. Waitressing continued as before on Friday and Saturday evenings. She continued to love all aspects of her work, but in her heart of hearts, what she still longed for was a full-time post with Snaith and Drew.

Her relationship with her flatmates continued to be good. They all looked forward to their social gatherings, and sometimes invited friends round to join them.

Phone calls with the family invariably brought interesting news, and there were no problems there at all. Jasmine kept Mum and Dad informed about the expansions to her farm office work and her teaching. Poppy kept asking what Bryony was doing. She also gave Jasmine detailed reports on how Tippy was taking to his new environment.

Yet, despite all of this being so right, there was something that was not. When she put her mind to it, all Jasmine could identify was a barely tangible sense of unease, and it seemed to be linked to her increasing habit of nibbling biscuits whenever she was in her room. She was sure that eating the biscuits wasn't *causing* the unease, but certainly the eating and the unease were connected in some way.

And then those stabbing pains in her abdomen started up again, particularly at night. They weren't there *every* night, but they were there often enough that Jasmine began to feel quite worried about them. They were sufficiently strong that they sometimes disturbed her sleep, and she found herself feeling irritable in the afternoons.

One day it occurred her that she might be upsetting her digestion by eating too many biscuits. She decided to stop eating them for a few days and see what happened. Although the disturbance lessened, it did not go away, and she noticed something else, too. Whereas in the past she would not have found any difficulty in changing what she ate, this time it was not the case. For the first time in her life, she found it very difficult indeed. In fact, she found that sitting in the evenings without nibbling biscuits left her feeling quite agitated, and she hunted around for something else. She took an apple from her kitchen cupboard, but although it was crunchy and tasted nice, eating it somehow didn't feel quite right. It didn't feel wrong, but it just did not satisfy her.

The next day she bought more biscuits, although now she decided to stick only to plain ones. Digestives seemed a good choice – one packet for her kitchen cupboard, and one for her room. That night passed without any discomfort, and the next morning she woke feeling refreshed. Believing that she had found the answer to her problems, she set off to work with a spring in her step.

Sometime over the following weeks, Jasmine became aware that the waistband of her skirt was tight, and slightly uncomfortable. Never mind, she thought, I expect I'm premenstrual. But the waistband not only remained tight, but also became even tighter. She tried on some of her other clothes, and found that she no longer had anything to wear that really fitted her. Jasmine began to sort through her things to see what could be altered. Her adjustments to Rosemary's dress had been very successful, and Rosemary had been able to wear it as planned.

In addition to making some of her existing clothes wearable again, Jasmine considered treating herself to something new. Feeling that she could now afford this, she spent some time the next Saturday afternoon going round the shops, choosing some comfortable items. In any case, she thought to herself, her wardrobe had needed revamping, and this was as good a time as any to get on with it. Her expanding waistline had prompted the review, and a lot of good had come out of that.

The only thing that didn't feel right was the quantity of biscuits that she consumed. Jasmine had tried various strategies to reduce her intake of them, but so far nothing had worked. Apples hadn't worked, and buying only plain biscuits hadn't worked. Next she had tried putting the start date on each packet, telling herself that she wasn't going to buy another packet for a certain number of days. But she always found herself finishing them sooner. In fact, if she were to be honest with herself, as time went on, each packet lasted for a shorter and shorter time.

She noticed that she began to look forward more than usual to the times when she was with the Greens. Then she began to realise that when she was there, she never thought about biscuits. And she became aware that when there was a plate of biscuits laid out, it never occurred to her to eat any of them.

The grumbling pains in her abdomen continued as before, almost every night, but she hadn't been aware of any more dreams. She told herself briskly that since nearly everything about her life was really good, why should she worry about a few extra biscuits and a night or two of discomfort?

It was when Jasmine noticed that she had consumed an entire packet of biscuits in one evening that she pulled herself up short. She promised herself that this was the last packet that would come into her room.

The following evening was difficult, very difficult indeed. Jasmine could not concentrate on anything that she had planned to do, and her mind was full of... biscuits. She tried pacing up and down the floor of her room, but this did not help at all. In fact, she felt that if only she paced along to the nearest corner shop, she would be able to get a packet of biscuits. Just a very small packet would do...

She was half way down the second flight of stairs before she remembered her resolve and retraced her steps. Back in the flat, she went straight to the kitchen. Perhaps there was the end of a packet out of sight at the back of her cupboard? She scrabbled around, checking everything, but there was no sign of any biscuits.

Sitting at the bare kitchen table, she contemplated her situation. The others were out, and she didn't expect them back until late. She was glad that they could not see her in this state.

Then a thought came into her head. Perhaps there were biscuits in the other cupboards? And if there were, surely her flatmates wouldn't mind if she had... just one?

Her hand was on the latch of Bryony's cupboard, and she was about to open the door, when she stopped.

'That will do you no good at all!' she said aloud, and she went back to her room, determined to concentrate on a book that she had borrowed from the local library. But before she picked up the book, she knew that it would not help. Instead she took her mobile phone out of her bag and keyed in Freya's number. There was no reply, so she left a voicemail: Hi, this is Jasmine. Need a chat. Hope you can ring later.

Strangely, this action had an almost immediate effect. Jasmine found herself able to pick up her book, and she lay down on her bed to read it.

It was more than an hour later when Jasmine's mobile rang.

She was so deeply absorbed in her reading that for a second or two she wondered what the noise was.

She grabbed the phone and found that it was Freya.

'I've got myself in a bit of a mess,' Jasmine began. 'Thanks for ringing back so soon.'

'What is it?' asked Freya, concerned.

Jasmine hesitated. 'Have you got time to talk now?'

'Yes, I have. I treated myself to something to eat on the way back from work. I had my phone with me, but I'd forgotten to switch it back on after I finished my shift.'

'I feel such an idiot,' Jasmine confessed.

'What about?'

'I'm addicted to... to eating biscuits,' Jasmine blurted out. The words sounded weird, but they were true. This was the first time that she had admitted it to herself.

'Well, thank goodness it isn't class A drugs!' Freya sounded quite relieved. 'Tell me what's been happening.'

Jasmine told her friend about how the nibbling had got completely out of hand, and how this evening she had been on the edge of taking food from her flatmates' cupboards.

'Poor you,' said Freya sympathetically. 'You must be feeling desperate.'

'I've never taken anything that isn't mine, and I was horrified when I found myself on the verge of it.'

'I'm sure they wouldn't have minded. If I were your flatmate, I certainly wouldn't.'

'But that's not the point. I don't want to take their biscuits, and I don't want to eat the wretched things anyway.' Jasmine was almost shouting. 'Oh, sorry,' she apologised.

'Don't worry,' Freya reassured her. 'But can you tell me why you're eating a lot of biscuits that you don't want to have?'

'No, I can't. If I had the answer to that, I don't think I'd be eating so many, and in that case I wouldn't be growing out of my clothes and contemplating theft.'

'Have you got any clues at all?'

'Not really. But when I'm at Restharrow Farm, I don't even notice the existence of biscuits.'

'That's interesting. There are bound to be plenty around.'

'Yes, I suppose it *is* interesting,' Jasmine agreed. 'I don't notice them even when they're right under my nose.'

'Well, I don't think we'll find a solution straight away,' Freya mused.

'I know, but actually, just the act of leaving you a message helped enough that I could read my book. Before that I felt as if I was climbing the walls.'

'I don't chain-eat biscuits, but I can sometimes go a bit funny around Smarties,' Freya confided.

'Smarties?' echoed Jasmine. 'You mean the coloured sweets? Poppy used to like those when she was small. She would arrange each colour in a different row, and then count how many of each colour she had. I taught her the names of colours and how to count.'

'She's so lucky to have had a big sister to help her with all that.'

'Freya, do you ever end up eating packet after packet of Smarties?' asked Jasmine.

'Not now, but I ate quite a lot for a while after Gran died.'

'I'm so glad you've told me about that. I feel I know you a bit more, and I don't feel as awful about the biscuit thing now. I can perfectly understand how after your Gran died you ended up clinging on to something that's as easy to get hold of as Smarties.'

'Sometimes I used to fall asleep clutching a pack of them, and in the morning I would have to pick them out of my bedding. I would scrabble about trying to find them all.'

'I wish you'd told me,' said Jasmine sympathetically.

'I went through a stage where I couldn't tell anybody much at all,' Freya told her. 'By the way, I should say that after I talked to Mum about my contact with Gran when I was small, something fell into place about Smarties.'

'What was that?'

'When Mum was going through what she remembered of her and me being at Gran's, she said that my Saturday treat in those holiday times was a packet of Smarties, and that when we went back home to Dad, he nearly always had a packet in his pocket for me.'

'That's amazing! Freya, that really explains why you found yourself clinging to them after your gran died.'

'Yes, I can see that now.'

Jasmine went on. 'It's a good thing we chatted about those times, and you decided to ask your mum some questions.'

'It's a good thing for me, and I think it's a good thing for you, too.'

'What do you mean?'

'It's because of that we know how important it is to find out what biscuits meant to you when *you* were small.'

'Oh...' Jasmine's voice trailed off. Then she murmured, 'I *see*.'

Neither Freya nor Jasmine spoke for a few minutes.

Then Jasmine said hesitantly, 'I suppose I should speak to Mum about this.'

'Correct.'

'But for some reason I don't want to.'

At first Freya said nothing. Then she said quietly, 'Maybe you'll have to think about that.'

'I'm definitely going to say something to Bryony and Rosemary quite soon, though.'

'That would be a good start,' Freya agreed. 'They're the sort of people its worth confiding in.'

Chapter Nineteen

Jasmine had felt a bit better after her conversation with Freya. When she next bought a packet of biscuits, she found that eating them felt different. She ate quite a few, but she didn't feel so desperate, and she noticed that it wasn't too difficult to take the decision to put the rest in a tin in her kitchen cupboard. After that she was able to relax with an interesting book about Spain. Maybe she would be able to save up to have a holiday with Maider next year...

A conversation with Bryony and Rosemary turned out better than she could have imagined. The thought that she had nearly stolen food from them had lingered on in her mind, and she felt inhibited about saying anything about her problem. However, a late breakfast one Saturday morning gave her an opportunity, from which she did not shy away.

It began with a light-hearted chat.

Perched on a kitchen stool, Bryony announced cheerfully, 'By the way, you two, I've got something to sit on now.'

This was self-evident. Jasmine and Rosemary stared at her, puzzled.

'Yes,' Bryony continued, 'for the first time in ages I've got a bit of padding on my bum.'

Rosemary's expression broke into a smile. 'That's great news. I hadn't been scrutinising you, but now you mention it, I can see that you don't look gaunt any more.'

'Slender, but not gaunt,' Jasmine added.

'It's the companionship that's done it,' Bryony explained. 'Although there were people around in the last flat, I felt more and more isolated there.'

'You'll have to keep an eye on that tendency,' Rosemary advised.

'Yes, indeed. The combination of working nearly all the time and the others heading off into the sunset with their partners certainly had a big impact on me. The trouble is that I couldn't see it at the time. It all built up quite slowly. There were no sudden big changes until the move here.'

'It's a good thing you were forced to move,' Rosemary observed. 'Otherwise you might have faded away.' This latter statement was delivered as if in fun, but Bryony read its message loud and clear.

'I've promised myself that I'll spot the signs early,' she replied. Then she stopped and thought for a minute or two before continuing. 'Actually, what I need to do is to keep my life in balance – working a bit less and seeing people a bit more. Then it can't happen again.'

Rosemary nodded. 'That sounds more like it.'

Jasmine had remained quiet throughout this conversation, but now she said, 'I'm in the middle of making some changes myself.' She didn't wait for a response, and barely pausing for breath blurted out, 'I was eating more and more biscuits.' Somehow she imagined that her friends could now see right through her, and knew that she had nearly taken their things. Feeling very uncomfortable, she flushed and added, 'I nearly ended up looking in your cupboards for some.'

Rosemary reached across and put her hand on Jasmine's arm. 'You're welcome to try any of my food.'

This response was so warm and genuine that tears pricked Jasmine's eyes.

'I don't usually buy biscuits, but you can certainly root around in my cupboard if you're short of something,' Bryony offered.

'That's really kind of you both.' Jasmine's voice wobbled a little as she said this. She swallowed and then continued. 'Both of you should feel the same about mine.'

'That's good to know,' said Rosemary. 'Thanks.'

'I like this arrangement,' Bryony reflected. 'In a way I wish we'd thought to set it up when we first moved in.'

'It's a good way to start the next phase, though,' Rosemary commented.

'Definitely,' agreed Bryony.

'Jasmine,' said Rosemary, 'there's something I'd like to ask.'

'Go ahead.'

'I could keep biscuits on or off my shopping list. Have you any preference?'

Again tears pricked Jasmine's eyes. Her friend was being so kind and understanding, and to begin with she didn't know quite what to say. 'Er...'

'You could think about it and let me know,' Rosemary offered. 'I had some odd tangles with food when I first left home, so I've got a bit of an idea of what things might feel like for you.'

'You, too!' exclaimed Jasmine. 'Freya was telling me about hers. I think that until then I was under the illusion I was the only one.' She laughed. 'How silly! Oh, I know that magazines are full of stories about binges and diets, but a lot of that never seems quite real.'

'I'm glad to say that for a long time I've not worried about my weight at all,' said Rosemary, 'and I've not felt stressed about what I eat. Sometimes I eat more and need bigger clothes for a while, and other times I eat less, and end up where I started. The main thing is that I enjoy food, and I'm not preoccupied by uncomfortable feelings about it.'

'Apart from my accidental starvation practices, I've had a brush with drinking a bit too much alcohol,' Bryony confided. 'I haven't done it for a long time, but I remember it could be pretty hairy.'

Jasmine gaped at her. 'Oh dear, how awful for you.'

'Well, it's all very much in the past now, I'm glad to say. Apart from any risks to health, it certainly depleted my

141

meagre bank balance, and of course that led to scrimping on my groceries.'

The conversation about food continued for a while, and then moved on to other subjects.

Before they parted, Rosemary said, 'Can we get together sometime to talk about overnight guests? I am clear about the rules laid down in the agreement I signed at the beginning, and I expect you've got the same version.'

'Surely that's all we need to take into account,' said Jasmine.

'Yes, and no,' replied Rosemary. 'Personally, I'd like to feel that you are both comfortable with any guest of mine being around, and so I'd like to talk about that.'

'I enjoyed Poppy's visits very much,' said Bryony, 'but in the end she didn't stay overnight.'

Rosemary continued. 'A friend of mine will be around next month. I'd like to offer him a bed for the occasional night or so, but I'd like to chat that over with both of you before I say anything to him.'

'Er... I don't want to appear nosey, but...' Bryony began.

Rosemary laughed. 'We've known each other for ages. We once had a kind of fling, but it wasn't really what either of us wanted. He's good company.'

'You should just go ahead,' Jasmine told her. She nudged Bryony. 'I'll make sure you don't forget to eat while he's around.'

Bryony smiled. 'That's good.' Then she turned to Rosemary and said, 'We'll look forward to meeting him.'

Chapter Twenty

In the days that followed, Jasmine began to plan her first visit to her family. She would stay for two nights – travelling there on a Saturday afternoon and returning on Monday evening. That way, all she had to do was cancel her Saturday evening waitressing and her Monday afternoon computing classes. She fixed the dates and found that she was looking forward to the trip very much. It would be great to see her family again, and looking round the house would be much better than relying solely on the photographs that she had seen.

The last packet of biscuits that she had bought lay at the back of her cupboard, unopened. She hardly noticed its existence, and when she did, its contents held no appeal. She found that she was sleeping better, too, and there was no more of that unpleasant abdominal pain. She was glad that she'd never mentioned it to Mum. There was no point in causing her unnecessary worry. Even when she saw Freya, she didn't mention it. There were always far more important things to talk about.

Two weekends later, Jasmine set off to catch the train. She took with her an overnight bag and a book to read on the way. Dad had promised to collect her at the station. He had told her that from there it was usually a twenty-minute drive back to the house.

The pleasant journey included the companionship of people of her own age, who were travelling to see friends for the weekend. They left the train a couple of stations before Jasmine, but by then she had given them her e-mail address so that they could keep in touch.

As the train drew alongside the platform, Jasmine spotted Dad, and then she saw Poppy, not far away. Neither of them had seen her, but as soon as she appeared out of the train, Poppy came running across to give her a hug. After that she didn't stop talking until they reached home. Dad had given Jasmine a hug and had taken her bag. He had winked at her, but had said nothing.

'We're nearly there now,' Poppy announced excitedly. 'It's at the other end of this street.'

Jasmine nodded. She thought that she could see Norrie and Blake leaning against a gatepost, and she soon found out that she was right.

When she got out of the car, the brothers said, 'Hi! See you around.' Then they walked off up the road.

But before she had reached the house, they turned back.

'That was just a joke,' Norrie explained.

'Yeah,' said Blake. 'Actually we're pleased to see you.' He was grinning from ear to ear.

Norrie nodded. 'Er... quite pleased.'

By now, Mum was standing at the opened front door. Her delight was very apparent. 'It's lovely speaking to you on the phone, dear,' she said as she hugged Jasmine, 'and seeing you again is absolutely wonderful.'

Poppy had allowed these fragments of interaction with the others, but now she tugged at Jasmine's arm and demanded loudly, 'Come and see Tippy's bed.'

'Everyone can meet in the kitchen,' said Mum. 'I'll put the kettle on, and I've baked a special cake.'

Poppy almost dragged Jasmine through the hallway to the back of the house where there was a large sunny porch. There, in one corner, Tippy was curled up in a basket. At the sound of voices, he pricked up one ear, opened his eyes, and without hesitation jumped straight into Jasmine's arms, purring loudly.

Jasmine laughed. 'I think he remembers me.'

Norrie came up quietly behind her and surprised her by

saying in a low voice, 'He's one of us. How could he forget?'

Blake joined him, but did not speak.

At the kitchen table, Poppy announced, 'I want to be the one who shows Jasmine round.'

'Well, you can't show her *our* room,' said Norrie and Blake together.

This stalled Poppy, although only temporarily. 'Okay.' She took a breath and then went on. 'Mum and Dad can show her round except for our rooms. You can do yours and I'll do mine.'

Norrie and Blake looked mildly surprised, but said nothing.

Then Blake turned to Jasmine and said, 'We're going out for a bit soon. We'll show you this evening.'

'That's fine. I'll look forward to it,' Jasmine replied.

After they had gone, Poppy chattered on for another half hour before Dad said, 'I think Mum and I will do our showing round now, and then I'd like you to help me to wash the car.'

Poppy pulled a face. After that, she announced that she would get everything ready, and disappeared.

Dad smiled at Jasmine. 'Shall we start with your police cell quarters?'

'Lead the way,' Jasmine replied.

When Dad opened the door to it, Jasmine gasped. 'It's beautiful!' she exclaimed. 'I'd no idea that somewhere with a dark past could end up looking so lovely.'

'Your dad's certainly made a wonderful job of it,' said her mother. 'It was progressing well, but when we knew that you would be coming, he was determined to get it finished.'

'Oh, thanks Dad!' said Jasmine, hugging him impulsively.

The rest of the house was much as she had seen from the original photographs, except that of course it was now furnished with things that were largely familiar to her.

Jasmine could understand why her parents had bought this house. It really was the kind of home that they wanted.

The car-cleaning job completed, Poppy seemed to have settled down quite a lot. She joined Mum and Jasmine in the sitting room where they were having a conversation about sewing, and for a while she sat quietly, listening. Tippy sneaked in, climbed on her knee and fell asleep.

Eventually, Poppy said, 'Do you think I can learn how to sew, too?'

'I don't see why not,' Mum replied.

'I'd like to make something to wear,' Poppy mused.

'We can have a chat about it soon,' Mum promised.

'I'll be interested to hear how this project goes,' said Jasmine. 'When you've got some idea of what you'll be making, have a look on the internet for material. There are some really good sites. I can send you some links if you want.'

Poppy bounced up and down excitedly. 'Hooray! Now come and look at my room.'

Carrying Tippy, Poppy led the way upstairs and threw the door to her room open.

'I chose the colours for the paint,' she explained proudly, '*and* I painted the whole of one wall myself.'

Jasmine congratulated her. 'You've done really well. The colours are nice, and I like the way you've arranged your furniture. It looks as if you might have a real eye for this kind of thing.'

Poppy looked pleased… very pleased. 'Well, then. I'll show you a secret. That is… if you promise not to tell.'

Without waiting for the promise, Poppy pulled out a large jotter and handed it to her sister. Feeling puzzled, Jasmine opened it and turned the pages. There she found a number of sketches of clothing.

'Poppy, these are really good!' she exclaimed. 'I'm so impressed.'

Poppy smiled. 'That means when I show them to Mum, she'll think they're okay, too.'

'She won't think they're okay,' said Jasmine seriously. 'She'll think they're very good.'

Poppy looked delighted. 'Then she's bound to teach me how to sew.'

The viewing of Norrie and Blake's room that evening was less remarkable. Jasmine learned that they had done most of the decorating themselves, albeit under Dad's supervision.

'We worked out that we might not be here full-time for all that long,' Norrie told her.

'But in any case we wanted to make it look good,' said Blake.

Jasmine's response was heartfelt. 'You've certainly achieved that.'

Sunday passed pleasantly. Jasmine had enjoyed her night in the former police cell, and over breakfast had joked about being surprised to find that the door wasn't locked. She spent some time in the morning helping Mum in the garden, and in the afternoon, Dad took everyone, except Norrie and Blake, to a country park about fifteen miles away.

Jasmine's train was due to leave at one fifteen on Monday. She made sure that she was up to say goodbye to her brothers and Poppy before they left for school. Mum had taken the morning off work. Dad had insisted on booking a taxi to take Jasmine to the station, so she and her mother were free to spend most of the morning together.

It was during this time that Jasmine found herself talking about Freya. Her mother showed obvious interest in the news of Freya's dilemma about her career path.

'I haven't seen her for ages, but I always like hearing how she's getting on,' she remarked. 'I remember so well when I first met her – after she'd come to live at her gran's during school terms. Do give her my love when you see her again.'

'Yes, of course I will. By the way, Mum, do you have any photos of when Norrie and Blake were babies and Dad looked after them so I could have a birthday party?'

'I might have. We can go and have a look in a minute. Wasn't that the first time I met Freya?'

'That's right. In fact Freya and I were remembering it quite recently.'

'You'll have noticed that we've got quite a lot stored in the cupboard under the stairs. That's the first place we should look for old photos.'

Soon they had pulled out several large cardboard boxes from the cupboard, and Mum was searching through them.

'Aha!' she said triumphantly. 'I think I'm getting warmer...' Then she added, 'It would have made it a lot easier if I'd labelled these.'

Jasmine picked up an album from several that Mum had put to one side. She started to turn the pages slowly. Here there were photos of herself as a baby and as a toddler.

'How sweet...' she mused half to herself.

Mum glanced across. 'Yes, you were a lovely little girl.' She paused, and then added, 'And you're still lovely, but of course you're a lot bigger.'

Jasmine turned another page. There were more photos of herself, now playing with her mother.

'I must have been about eighteen months old in that picture,' she murmured.

Her mother glanced across. 'That's about right,' she agreed.

'You've got a bit of a bulge at the front,' Jasmine remarked. Thinking of her recent struggle with biscuits, she asked, 'Had you been eating Mars bars or something?'

Her mother kept looking through the boxes. It was as if she hadn't heard what Jasmine had said.

Jasmine glanced across and noticed that her mother was

a bit pale.

She reached across and touched her arm saying, 'Mum, are you okay?'

'Er... I've so enjoyed seeing you here... I'll miss you.'

'I'm so taken up with finding my way in life that I'm usually preoccupied with that,' said Jasmine honestly. 'But I've noticed that when I'm staying overnight at Restharrow Farm I feel more myself. I think it's because being there reminds me of being with you all when I was younger.'

'I can understand that very well,' her mother replied. 'When I was in the process of leaving home I was much the same.'

Jasmine found this exchange helpful, but she could see that her mother still didn't look all right.

'Mum, is there something else?' she asked quietly.

Her mother seemed to freeze, but then she turned to Jasmine and said, 'Yes, there's something else. Let's sit down with a cup of tea, and I'll tell you what it is. Will apple and blackcurrant be all right for you?'

Seated opposite each other at the kitchen table, Jasmine waited.

Her mother looked straight into her eyes and said, 'Jasmine, I was pregnant in that photograph.'

Jasmine felt stunned, and she didn't know what to say.

Her mother went on. 'It was an accidental pregnancy, but your dad and I were pleased and excited when we found out. I was at four months when I miscarried. I'd been carrying twins. I haemorrhaged quite badly and had to be in hospital. When I got home I was quite weak at first, and of course I was in a state of shock. The whole thing left your dad and I even more grateful that we had you, our beautiful little daughter. We decided that we were going to be very careful that I wouldn't get pregnant again for some time. That's why there's quite a big gap between you and your brothers.'

'Mum, I don't know what to say...' Jasmine began,

'except that I'm really glad you told me. I'm not sure that I'm taking it in properly yet, though.'

Her mother was looking less pale now, and she reached across the table to take Jasmine's hand, saying, 'I expect that'll take time.'

They hadn't found the party photos before Jasmine left, but her mother promised to keep looking for them.

As she climbed into the taxi, Jasmine called, 'Tell Poppy I'll send those links to her soon.'

Chapter Twenty-one

Jasmine was due to see Freya again the following Monday evening. She sent a text to say she'd got back and that she was looking forward to seeing her. Jasmine's work diary was almost full until then, and the days seemed to fly past.

On Saturday a letter came from Mum. In it Jasmine found two copies of a photograph of herself and Freya at the birthday party. The handwritten note said: Will keep looking in case there are more.

'That was good of Mum to get these to me so quickly,' Jasmine murmured. 'I'll be able to give Freya hers soon.'

When Jasmine arrived at Freya's place on Monday evening, she was surprised when Freya beckoned her in saying, 'Change of plan. The others are away for a couple of nights so we may as well lounge around here with our feet up. I've got something bubbling away in the kitchen. Should be ready soon.' She disappeared off for a minute. Jasmine hung up her coat and waited.

When Freya returned, Jasmine took an envelope out of her bag and handed it to her. 'Present from Mum,' she said. 'And she sends her love as well.'

Freya took the envelope and opened it. A smile spread across her face when she saw the photograph. 'Aren't we sweet!' she exclaimed. 'And those dresses...'

'If she finds any more she'll send them on,' Jasmine told her. 'Freya, I've got some news...'

'What is it?'

'Mum miscarried twins when I was eighteen months old. Apparently she was quite ill and was in hospital,' Jasmine blurted out.

'Oh, wow! That's pretty bad,' said Freya. 'How awful for you.'

'Well, it was awful for her and Dad,' Jasmine corrected her.

'It would be really bad for you,' Freya insisted. 'You would be too young to grasp most of what was happening around you. Do you know who looked after you?'

'I haven't a clue,' Jasmine replied. 'I didn't think to ask.'

'How did it come out?'

'It was when we were looking for photos of that party. I came across one of me at eighteen months and I commented to Mum that she must have been eating more at the time. She looked a bit bulged out, and she never usually does. She went pale, and it was after that she told me.'

'I imagine there's more to be talked about, but maybe not yet,' Freya commented. 'In any case, keep me informed.'

'I certainly will.'

'I've got a bit of news, too,' Freya confided, 'although it's not as stunning as yours. I'll just get our food and then we can get settled.'

She was soon back with two large bowls on a tray, together with spoons.

'I hope this'll do,' she said apologetically. 'Right, I've got two bits of news. One is that I'm thinking of going out with someone – someone I met at work.' Without giving Jasmine time to ask questions, she rushed on, 'And for now I'm not planning to change my job. Er... his name's Russell, and he's working in the stroke unit. Actually we met the day after you helped me to escape the clutches of the horrible Mick.'

Jasmine sensed that Freya wasn't ready to discuss any of this. In between mouthfuls of her supper she said, 'I'm glad you told me. Let me know how it goes.'

'I will,' Freya replied. 'I mean, I want to.'

'By the way, can I ask you a medical question?' Jasmine asked.

'Of course. Go on.'

'I've had some bad stabbing pains in my abdomen at night. I haven't had any for the last few weeks, though. I think they're something to do with being stressed.'

'Well, you can't bank on that,' Freya advised. 'A trip to your GP wouldn't be a bad idea.'

'Even though I'm not getting the pains at the moment?'

'It's up to you. But promise me one thing.'

'What's that?'

'If the pains come back again, you'll make an appointment straight away.'

Jasmine saw the sense in this and agreed.

The conversation then went on to discussing a book that they had both been reading, and planning when to go to see a particular film together.

'I feel really relaxed this evening,' Freya remarked. She was lounging backwards with her bare feet on the coffee table, and she wiggled her toes around. 'I'll tell you more about Russell if it comes to anything.'

Jasmine nodded. In the past Freya had had some painful disappointments in the romantic side of her life. Jasmine wondered how her other friends would fare. Bryony and Rosemary seemed more keen on building their careers, and Maider was still recovering from the loss of Tim. Perhaps her trip to see Stephan and Clover would open things up a bit. Jasmine herself had always enjoyed male company, and she knew that she wanted a family of her own, but she, too, was taken up with building her career.

By the end of the evening, Freya had dozed off. Not wanting to disturb her, Jasmine made her way quietly to the kitchen and did the clearing up. Then she wrote a note for Freya, covered her with a blanket and crept out of the flat.

Chapter Twenty-two

The following week, a phone chat with Mum ended on a mysterious note. She had just finished telling Jasmine about some more photographs that she planned to send.

'I've written you a letter,' she said. 'I decided I'd rather do that than send an e-mail or say something in a phone chat. Let me know when it arrives. If you want to talk about it later, you only have to ask.'

'Thanks, Mum,' Jasmine replied. She would look forward to seeing her mother's familiar handwriting.

In the end she didn't have long to wait, as the letter arrived three days later. She opened it straight away.

Dear Jasmine,

Over the years since I miscarried the first twins, I have sometimes felt sad about how we couldn't support you through that time in the way we would have liked to. I kept an eye open in case you showed signs of distress, but apart from some entirely understandable tears at the beginning, you never did.

When I was taken to hospital, we had to leave you with the family who lived next door. They were kind people and you were used to seeing them around, although you'd never stayed with them before. They had three children who were all primary school age. Dad visited you there whenever he could, but he had me in hospital and was overloaded at work, so you didn't see all that much of him.

There was one night when the neighbours couldn't have you, and Dad had to take you to his office. He managed to get you to sleep in your buggy. He stayed up working and then slept on the floor for a few hours.

The family from next door moved away the following year, and we lost touch with them.

I think that when you were staying with them they gave you biscuits, because after I came home you asked for biscuits a lot. We used to choose a packet together whenever we were at the supermarket, although as time went on you lost interest in them.

Love, Mum xx

A smile spread slowly across Jasmine's face. Without her having to ask anything, Mum had told her what her biscuit-eating meant. When she had been small, as well being something to eat, biscuits could be relied upon to be there for her while she was separated from her parents. As an adult, the pattern had re-emerged when she was again separated from her parents while under various stresses. Confiding to her friends about her struggles with biscuits had increased the trust between them, and when she and her mother searched through family photographs, her early trauma had begun to come to light.

* * * * *

Jasmine wondered what the next year would hold for her. Maybe she would have a holiday in Spain with Maider. And maybe a full-time job with Snaith and Drew would become available…

Life felt full of promise.

Titles from Augur Press

Self-help novellas
by Mirabelle Maslin
Miranda	£6.99	978-0-9558936-5-0
Lynne	£6.99	978-0-9558936-6-7
Field Fare	£6.99	978-0-9558936-8-1

Trilogy by Mirabelle Maslin
Beyond the Veil	£8.99	978-0-9549551-4-4
Fay	£8.99	978-0-9549551-3-7
Emily	£8.99	978-0-9549551-8-2

Other novels
One Eye Open: Can a Dolphin Save the World? by Steve Cameron	£7.99	978-0-9571380-1-8
The Candle Flame by Mirabelle Maslin	£7.99	978-0-9558936-1-2
Letters to my Paper Lover by Fleur Soignon	£7.99	978-0-9549551-1-3

For children and young people
The Supply Teacher's Surprise by Mirabelle Maslin	£5.99	978-0-9558936-4-3
Tracy by Mirabelle Maslin	£6.95	978-0-9549551-0-6
The Fifth Key by Mirabelle Maslin	£7.99	978-0-9558936-0-5

Child development
Infants and children: An introduction to emotional development by Mirabelle Maslin	£7-99	978-0-9571380-2-5
The Human Being by Dr W N Taylor	£7.99	978-0-9571380-3-2

Eating disorder
Size Zero and Beyond: £13.99   978-0-9571380-0-1
A personal study of anorexia
nervosa by Jacqueline M Kemp

Hemiplegia
Hemiplegic Utopia: Manc Style   £6.99   978-0-9549551-7-5
  by Lee Seymour

Sexual Abuse
Carl and other writings   £5.99   978-0-9549551-2-0
  by Mirabelle Maslin

Health
Mercury in Dental Fillings   £5.99   978-0-9558936-2-9
  by Stewart J Wright
Lentigo Maligna Melanoma: £5.99   978-0-9558936-9-8
A sufferer's tale
  by Mirabelle Maslin

Miscellaneous
On a Dog Lead   £6.99   978-0-9549551-5-1
  by Mirabelle Maslin

*   *   *   *

Poetry

The Poetry Catchers by pupils from Craigton Primary School	£7.99	978-0-9549551-9-9
Poems of Wartime Years by W N Taylor	£4.99	978-0-9549551-6-8
The Voice Within by Catherine Turvey	£5.99	978-0-9558936-3-6
Now is where we are by Hilary Lissenden	£6.99	978-0-9558936-7-4
Along Love's Pathway by Hamnah Maynard	£6.99	978-0-9571380-5-6
Poems from a Family Man by John Marshall	£6.99	978-0-9571380-6-3
Patterns of perception by Ken Simpson	£6.99	978-0-9571380-7-0
Girl in the Mirror by Alicja Kuberska	£6.99	978-0-9571380-8-7

Ordering:
Online   **www.augurpress.com**

By Post   Delf House, 52, Penicuik Road, Roslin,
Midlothian EH25 9LH UK

Postage and packing: £2.00 for each book, and add £0.75p for each additional item.

Cheques payable to Augur Press. Prices and availability subject to change without notice. When placing your order, please indicate if you do not wish to receive any additional information.

Miranda by Mirabelle Maslin

ISBN 978·0·9558936·5·0   £6.99

Newly unemployed, Miranda is feeling directionless and dejected. Then she encounters Kate, a former work colleague. Kate is now facing redundancy. Their friendship is rekindled, and as the two women share their problems and dilemmas, they begin to confide about experiences that have affected their lives.

This is the first book in a series of self-help fiction titles.

By reading about the lives of fictional characters, the reader learns much about how to unravel present day problems. The understanding of stresses that began in childhood years casts light on why the characters are struggling with the difficulties that they are having now.

Order from your local bookshop, amazon.co.uk or the augurpress website at www.augurpress.com

Lynne by Mirabelle Maslin

ISBN 978-0-9558936-6-7   £6.99

Victimised by the new office manager and worried about her mother's health, Lynne feels at a very low ebb. When she decides to be more open with her mother about her concerns, she is surprised to find that they both benefit.

Lynne's mother is determined to help her daughter explore why she had lost interest in finding a partner for herself, and she approaches the subject sensitively. Thus supported, Lynne faces the challenge of preparing to look for a new relationship.

Together Lynne and her mother take a number of positive steps that lead to change and enrichment of their lives.

Order from your local bookshop, amazon.co.uk or the augurpress website at www.augurpress.com

Field Fare by Mirabelle Maslin

ISBN 978-0-9558936-8-1   £6.99

Deep in the Cheshire countryside, Philip Thornton has created 'Field Fare' - a hotel with a special reputation for its game dishes. The building contains a secret, known only to Philip. Feeling lonely while her husband, Grant, is away, Teresa dines at 'Field Fare', and Philip entices her to sample a unique cordial. When Teresa confides about her experience to Carrie, her young hairdresser, she learns that Carrie has had a similar encounter. Could there be more? Concerned, Teresa approaches her friend, Monica. Aided by Grant, they devise a plan...

Order from your local bookshop, amazon.co.uk or the augurpress website at www.augurpress.com

Infants and children
An introduction to emotional development
by Mirabelle Maslin

Paperback:
ISBN 978·0·9571380·2·5
£7.99

Kindle edition:
ISBN 978·0·9571380·4·9
£3.54

A parent's ability to be able to see and understand things through the eyes of their child is fundamental. The child will come to feel truly known by the parent, and the parent helps him to make sense of what surrounds him. And where can true comfort be found? True comfort arises from the knowledge of relationship that is based on trust. And what about the needs of the child of the past that dwells inside each 'adult' state? This book opens up a whole new world of understanding for parents and carers.

For more information including an excerpt and an interview with the author visit:

www.infantsandchildren.co.uk

Order from your local bookshop, amazon.co.uk or the augurpress website at www.augurpress.com

MIRANDA
Mirabelle Maslin

LYNNE
Mirabelle Maslin

Field Fare
~
Mirabelle Maslin

BEYOND THE VEIL

MIRABELLE
MASLIN

FAY Mirabelle
Maslin

Mirabelle Maslin
EMILY

——————— * *This is a trilogy* * ———————

Letters to my Paper Lover
FLEUR SOIGNON

The Candle Flame
Mirabelle Maslin

**ONE
EYE OPEN**
CAN A DOLPHIN SAVE THE WORLD?

STEVE CAMERON

The Supply
Teacher's
Surprise
Mirabelle Maslin

Mirabelle
Maslin

tracy

from the author of Beyond the Veil

THE FIFTH KEY
Mirabelle Maslin

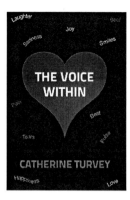

THE VOICE WITHIN

CATHERINE TURVEY

Poems of Wartime Years
W N Taylor

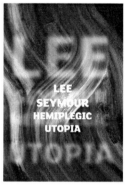

LEE
SEYMOUR
HEMIPLEGIC
UTOPIA

Now Is Where We Are
Hilary Lissenden

JACQUELINE M KEMP
Size Zero & Beyond
A personal study of anorexia nervosa

Mirabelle Maslin
CARL AND OTHER WRITINGS

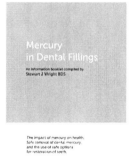

Mercury
in Dental Fillings

An information booklet compiled by
Stewart J Wright BDS

The impact of mercury on health,
Safe removal of dental mercury,
and the use of safe options
for restoration of teeth.

LENTIGO
MALIGNA
MELANOMA:
A sufferer's tale

MIRABELLE MASLIN

Mirabelle Maslin
ON A DOG LEAD

Poems from a
FAMILY MAN

JOHN MARSHALL

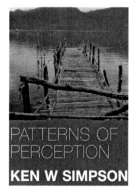

PATTERNS OF
PERCEPTION

KEN W SIMPSON

Mirabelle Maslin

Infants and children
An introduction to
emotional development

HANNAH MAYNARD
Along love's pathway

ALICJA MARIA KUBERSKA
GIRL IN THE MIRROR

The Human Being
Understanding and treatment of the person
Dr W Norman Taylor

Lightning Source UK Ltd.
Milton Keynes UK
UKOW03f2258130217
294335UK00001B/94/P